Zensational Mysteries

Zensational Mysteries

Amazing Mythology & Urban Legends. Looking for answers; what is real?

Rahul Karn

Rahul Karn

CONTENTS

ZENSATIONAL MYSTERIES

Amazing Mythology & Urban Legends.
Looking for answers; what is real?

Rahul Karn

<u>Dedicated To</u>
The Buddha
(The Enlightened One)

<u>**PREFACE**</u>

Dear Zen Friends,

Science says that the universe is expanding. Our knowledge of the universe and related phenomena are also expanding day by day. But in spite of the enormous leap of science, there are still many phenomena that have puzzled scientists and experts.

Zen Masters are known to do mysterious acts with their disciples. Sometimes they say weird kinds of stuff, sometimes they shout, sometimes say non-sensical things to shock and awaken the students. Earlier, people used to think that they were mere nonsense. But with time, when Zen entered mainstream science, psychologists started to study mindfulness and then all that the Zen Masters did begin to make sense. Then people started to find meanings behind those weird sayings.

The scientific aspect of Zen was most interesting to me because the Zen Masters used to awaken students without giving any dogma or faith system. They used to prescribe meditation to the students, which is a scientific activity. It is not against science.

Despite this scientific aspect, I sometimes used to encounter certain Zen Stories which contained unbelievable magical incidents. I used to call them magical because they seemed to be anti-scientific to me. I used to ignore such stories and didn't use to share them often with my readers.

But recently, I came to know about some scientific research on such supernatural incidents that made me think that the Zen Masters were really visionary people who had deep insight into the nature of things as they are. This book tries to bring the mysterious aspects of those Zen Masters and some unsolved mysteries together. I am not going to solve the mysteries. I am merely putting those mysteries from the various viewpoints of scientists and alternative theorists to the readers, which will bridge the gap between science and mythology. I don't have any intention to make my readers believe in those scientific or alternative theories. My idea is that merely acknowledging those unsolved mysteries will make you befriend those so-called magical Zen Stories as well.

There was a demand from my readers to provide a commentary on Zen Stories. I have read thousands of Zen Stories and writing commentaries on so many stories is beyond my time availabilities. In this edition, I have tried to give a short interpretation of the stories as well, which makes the book even more helpful.

Should you have any queries, please don't hesitate to contact me on zensationalstories@gmail.com.

Have a Zensational time!

Your Zen Friend,

Rahul Karn
Canberra, Australia
4th of October 2021

ZEN LEGENDS

1

THE MYSTERY

There was a question asked: "What is the further mystery in the mystery?"

Zen Master Tung-shan answered, "It is like the tongue of a dead man.".

~ Original Teachings of Chan Buddhism ~
~ Chang Chung Yuan ~

Lao Tzu, in his magnum opus Tao Te Ching, has said that we mould clay into a pot, but it is the emptiness inside that makes the vessel worthwhile. He continues: "Cut doors and windows for a room. But in its nothingness/emptiness is found the room's utility. So, the profit of existences is only for the sake of non-existences, where all the use is found to be." Lao Tzu's quote is very prominent. It is deep. He is saying that you don't live in a wall, rather inside the hollow, empty space created by the walls. You mould the clay to make a pot. But you don't put things inside the clay; rather, you put stuff inside the hollow space created by the clay.

Lao Tzu's saying looks like a profound philosophy, but such is life. The world progresses by the accumulation of knowledge, but life becomes liveable because of the mysteries. Understand this! Science progresses because of the fear of the unknown. There are so many things outside – the vast array of planets and celestial beings are lying overhead. There are many houses, plants, things and people around you. If all of them are unknown, it creates anxiety in the beings. So, science takes the route of labelling all things and phenomena. It merely gives a name to all the things and processes. But see yourself: does the labelling solves the mystery? If I give you a flower in your hand, you might be able to label it. But tell me, just by knowing the flower's name can you say that you have known it? No! The existence is a mystery, and that mystery has to be enjoyed. It can't be known.

Why am I saying that the mystery can't be known? Science tries to explain a certain aspect of the unknown by labelling it. When you ask about any labelled item, say moon, it can explain using another term. To explain, say A, it uses the term B. If you ask about B, it uses the term C and so on. If you go on asking about them, then the scientist will take you to Z, but if you ask further, the scientist will have to confess that further research is going about Z, and they don't know much about it. What kind of knowledge is this? Scientists explain A using B, B using C and so on, and Z is not known, then how can they say that A is known!?!

It happened so; a customer went to a gift shop to buy a hair clip for his wife. The shopkeeper gave him a beautiful hair clip for $10. Then the customer changed his mind and said that he would like to buy a nail-clipper for his wife. So, the shopkeeper replaced the hair clip with the nail-clipper. But the customer again changed his mind and decided to buy a gift card for her wife. So, the shopkeeper replaced the item and gave him a bill of $10 for the gift card. The customer said that he bought the gift card in place of a nail clipper. The shopkeeper said then asked to pay $10 for the nail-clipper. The customer said, "But I bought the nail-clipper instead of the hair clip." The shopkeeper demanded $10 for the hairclip. In the end, the customer says, "But I didn't buy the hairclip. So why should I pay?"

You will laugh at this joke, but this is how science works. It explains A using B, B using C and C using Z, but Z is unknown. What kind of knowledge is this?

Don't get me wrong. I am not saying that science is futile. I am saying that the knowledge acquired by science is utilitarian. It has a practical use, but it is not the ultimate truth. The existence is a mystery. That mystery has to be enjoyed and lived. It can't be fully known. That day will be very unfortunate when everything is known. There will be so much boredom in the world that everyone will commit suicide. This is the fact Zen Master Tung-Shan is saying in the above case. He is saying that a dead man has a tongue, but he can't speak. Similarly, the mystery is there, but it can't explain anything. It is simply there.

All the progress of science so far is merely the tip of the iceberg. There are many things in the world that are not known yet. There are many mysteries in the world that remain unsolved to date. Throughout the world, a specific type of megalithic monument is present, which has baffled archaeologists for eons. They were built using gigantic blocks of stone. Those stones weighing tons were fitted together without any cement or mortar in a polygonal style. Those fittings were so excellent that they interlocked the heavy blocks. Surprisingly, not even a blade can be fitted between them! Those interlocked walls were so advanced that they were earthquake-proof and shockproof! Ordinarily, traditional mainstream archaeologists say that modern tools were not available thousands of years ago. But it is impossible that with ordinary technologies, ancients built such structures. Examples of such constructions are present in Tiahuanaco, Ollantaytambo, Monte Alban, Rujm El-Hiri and Stonehenge.

One more baffling thing is that in many such places, the rocks were not present in the vicinity of such a structure. They were quarried from distant locations. It is unknown how they transported and lifted such huge rocks because the mechanical cranes which are available today were not present then.

You might have heard about the Mystery of Nimrud. Nimrud is an ancient place in Iraq. After 1854 lot of excavations were done there, and few very ancient carvings were found. In those carvings of men like people with feathers. They look like aliens. The thing that has baffled the experts is that a watch like an object is present in their wrists.

(Image taken from Wikipedia, Nimrud Page)

How can a watch be present in a structure which is at least 2,800 years old? Are they aliens? No one knows!

Rujm el-Hiri is an ancient monument consisting of concentric circles of stones. It is made of more than 42 thousand basalt rocks arranged in a circular fashion. The outermost wall is 520 ft in diameter and 8 feet high. They are around 5 thousand years old! Some of the stones weigh around 40 thousand tons which can't be lifted by even modern lifting machines! How people managed to bring such heavy rocks there?

The beauty of the site can't be seen from the ground. It can only be seen from a helicopter. But 5 thousand years ago, was a helicopter there? We have built aeroplanes in the last century only! Who made it? Why did he build it? No one knows! One theory says that aliens made it.

In classic Zen stories and religious texts, you will find many kinds of stuff that look supernatural, and thus, they are categorized as mythological. But when you start looking at these unsolved mysteries, those stories will begin making sense to you.

So, let's start our journey!

2

LIFE AFTER LIFE

When the Buddha was in the world, he once went to a layman's house to accept offerings.

In the house, there was a dog that stayed under the bed, day and night. He wouldn't allow anyone except members of the family to get near the bed. Anyone else who approached it got bitten. Even the Buddha was not allowed near the bed. The household experimented to see if the dog would bite the Buddha, and, sure enough, it snapped at him. They asked the Buddha why the dog was so protective of the bed. The Buddha said, 'Don't you know? In its last life, the dog was your father. Your father spent his whole life earning about three hundred ounces of gold and loved it so much he buried it under the bed. Then suddenly he got sick and died before he could tell you what he had done with it. After his death, he hurried right back as a dog to guard the pile of gold. If you don't believe me, start digging and you'll find the gold.'

They dragged the dog away and did, in fact, uncover exactly three hundred ounces of gold.

~ Buddha Root Farm by Hsuan Hua ~

Ordinarily, people explain this story by saying that the moral is that one should not be too attached to anything; otherwise, that attachment will bring misery. Since the story has elements of reincarnation, it is ruled out as a mythological story. People think that such stories are not true; rather, such stories are made up to impart some kind of wisdom to the audience.

Reincarnation has been a much-disputed topic in the world since time unknown. Earlier it used to be a matter of belief. Some people believe that life exists after death, while others don't.

The logic of non-believers is clear. When a person dies clinically, his body is either buried or burnt. In either case, nothing survives the death, and thus there should be no possibility of rebirth.

But in the past 50 years, science has made a lot of progress. A branch of psychology called parapsychology has evolved, which studies the cases which serve as evidence of the fact that the consciousness continues to move into a different body even after death. How it happens is not clear, but after examining hundreds of such cases, one thing is sure that it happens.

For thousands of years, many ancient civilizations have believed in reincarnation. The pyramids made by ancient Egyptians suggest that their history is more than four thousand years old! In the ancient scriptures of Hindus called Puranas, there are numerous cases of rebirth. The scriptures of Hindus talk about Punarjunma – which translates loosely to rebirth – and Punarmrityu, which means re-death. They also talk about Moksha, which means freedom from rebirth and re-death. This concept of consciousness transmigration has perpetuated in Buddhism and Jainism, other ancient religions of India. The Taoists also told stories of reincarnation. When Buddhism went to China and merged with Taoism to form Zen, many such stories of reincarnation were told.

In the modern age, William James, the founder of modern psychology, started to investigate reincarnation. In the past fifty years, many psychologists began to investigate the cases of rebirth in a scientific manner. The pioneer of Past Life Research was Dr Ian

Stevenson (1918-2007), a Canadian Psychiatrist from the department of Psychiatry in the University of Virginia.

Dr Ian Stevenson was fascinated with the cases of rebirth. In 1960, he published a paper titled 'The Evidence for Survival from Claimed Memories of Former Incarnations'. Chester Carlson, the inventor of the photocopier (Xerox) and his religious wife, became too interested in the research paper of Dr Ian Stevenson. Chester asked Stevenson whether he had personally investigated the cases. Stevenson said that such research was not considered scientific, and thus the universities didn't fund such investigations. Chester financed the trips of Dr Ian Stevenson, and he went to India and Sri Lanka to meet such reincarnated people.

Later on, Stevenson was appointed chairman of the department of psychiatry at the University of Virginia. Before dying, Chester left 1 million dollars for the University of Virginia to continue researching past lives. Carlson's donation helped Stevenson continue his research into reincarnation, and he documented several such cases where people remembered their past lives. He established DOPS (the Division of Personality Studies) at the University of Virginia. This department was solely for the research of parapsychology: the study of previous lives, near-death experiences and other paranormal phenomena.

Dr Stevenson spent an enormous amount of time and money travelling in South America, Lebanon, West Africa and South-East Asia in order to personally meet the cases who remembered their past lives. He documented the verified evidence as well! His most famous books are 'Children Who Remember Previous Lives: A Question of Reincarnation', 'Twenty Cases Suggestive of Reincarnation' and 'European Cases of the Reincarnation Type'.

He successfully brought reincarnation into the mainstream scientific research area. Now reincarnation is not a matter of belief. It is a scientifically verified phenomenon.

I will present few cases researched and documented by Ian Stevenson.

Case 1: The Weird Case of Captain Robert Snow

Robert Snow was a retired Captain of the Indianapolis Metropolitan Police Department, who in his career was in charge of the department of the Homicide and Robbery and the department of Organized Crime. The story begins at a party where Captain Snow meets a police psychologist who talks about past life regression techniques and cases. Captain didn't believe in reincarnation, so he denied the sayings of the psychologist. But the psychologist challenged him to go through past life regression himself, which the captain consented.

During the regression, the captain had a vivid visualization of himself as a painter painting a hunchback woman. To prove that it was not his past life and merely an imagination, he started to do investigations by visiting art galleries and contacted art dealers. But all was in vain, and when he came to a dead-end, he happily concluded that reincarnation doesn't exist.

One day accidentally, he went to an art gallery in the French Quarter of New Orleans. There he saw the same painting which he had seen during past life regression. He luckily found the name of the painter 'Carroll Beckwith'.

He, later on, accepted the fact of reincarnation and wrote a book on his own case of past life. The book is "Looking for Carroll Beckwith: The True Stories of a Detective's Search for His Past Life". It is available on Amazon! His case was researched and documented by Prof. Ian Stevenson.

Case 2: The Weird Case of Titu Singh

This story was first broadcast in 1990 on the BBC TV news program Forty Minutes.

In December 1983, a boy named Titu Singh was in a village near Agra. In his childhood, he used to talk about TV and radio. In the beginning, his parents didn't notice his weird sayings, but later on, he started to say that in his past life, he was Suresh Verma and his wife's name was Uma Devi. He also said that he used to own a radio shop in Agra. He recalled that in his past life, he was shot dead was a businessman called Sedickk Johaadien. There was a birthmark on his head, which he claimed was because he was shot dead.

When his brother started to investigate, he found that there was really a place called Suresh Radios and is owned by a widow called Uma Devi. Titu's brother took him to Uma Devi, and he revealed many things which only Suresh Verma and Uma Devi knew!

When this case was brought to light, the police started its investigation. Suresh's autopsy report revealed that the bullet had entered Suresh's head at exactly that place. Where the bullet had exited Suresh's head, there was a mole on Titu's head at the same location. When Agra police questioned the murderer, he confessed to the crime!

There are many more such cases on reincarnation. Those who want to do a scientific investigation should read the books by Prof. Ian Stevenson.

Case 3: The Weird Case of Taru Jarvi

Some people think that reincarnation is a psychological distortion where people born in Asia start believing that they are reincarnated because their religions psychologically condition them. This case is from Helsinki, Finland, where Taru Jarvi, a girl, was born on

27 May 1976. The parents of this girl were Heikki Jarvi and his wife, Iris.

At the age of around one and a half years, Taru started to speak and told her mother that her actual name was Jaska. This was surprising to Iris because Jaska was the nickname of her ex-husband Jaako Vuorenlehto, who had been run over and killed by a bus a few years ago. When questioned, Taru did indeed mention the incident. She said: "The vehicle was big. First, her stomach died and then the head!"

Stevenson personally met Taru and investigated the incident. He found that the descriptions of Taru were perfectly matching with the actual incident!

Taru didn't like her father, and she even said to him, "We don't need you here, you should go away."

She had many manly interests. She also had a preference for boy's clothes and kinds of stuff. Stevenson concluded that she was the re-birth of Jaako Vuorenlehto.

There are numerous such cases that have been verified by psychologists. Currently, Prof. Jim B. Tucker is a child psychiatrist and Bonner-Lowry Professor of Psychiatry and Neurobehavioral Sciences at the University of Virginia School of Medicine. His main research interests are documenting stories of children he claims remember previous lives and natal and prenatal memories. He is the author of Life Before Life: A Scientific Investigation of Children's Memories of Previous Lives, which presents an overview of over four decades of reincarnation research at the Division of Perceptual Studies. If you want to know about more recent cases, you must watch the documentary 'Survinging Death' available on Netflix. All such claims can't be co-incidences or hallucinations. In such cases, many remarkable features have been noted:

1. In most of the studied cases, a tragic or premature death occurred in the past life.
2. The child started to communicate about their past life right from childhood.
3. The gender of current life could be the same or even different from the past life.
4. The information provided by the child were investigated, and they were found to be matching with the actual past life incidents.
5. There were some physical signs which suggested continuity between the past and present lives. Many times, the habits and personality traits had a remarkable similarity.
6. Former relationships were continued.
7. The memories had a vast impact on the current life.

The 21 Grams Experiment

In 1907 Duncan MacDougall, a physician from Massachusetts, performed a weird scientific study. He weighed a man who was about to die. Once the man died, he weighed the dead body again. The dead weighed 21 grams less than the alive one. He performed the experiment again and again and concluded that the weight of the soul is 21 grams!

Hopefully, these cases have opened your eyes, and the story which we read in the beginning of the chapter would not feel too far-fetched. Obviously, since we can't talk to animals, we can't ask and verify whether it was a human being in its past life, but the possibility can't be ruled out. If gender could change in new life, why can't a human being be born as an animal in his next life?

There are many Zen stories and mythological anecdotes about reincarnation, but I am ending this chapter with a wonderful story from Dharma Master Thich-Thien-Tam from his book 'Buddhism of Wisdom and Faith for Pure Land Principles and Practice':

"Once there were two famous Zen Masters who had been awakened to the Way. One day, as they sat in meditation together, the young master had a thought of lust and desire, which he immediately severed. However, the Elder Master, seated opposite, already knew of the occurrence. After emerging from meditation, the Elder Master composed a poem, intending to tease his friend. The latter, sad and ashamed, immediately "gathered up his vital energy," and expired on the spot. The Elder Master, filled with remorse, called his disciples together and followed his friend in death, leaving these parting words: "My friend, while in meditation, had a false thought of lust and desire and will therefore certainly be entangled in love relationships in his next life. He died while unhappy with me, and therefore, upon rebirth, will cause havoc to the community of monks. I am partly responsible for all of this, so if I do not follow and guide him, I will not escape the consequences ..."

The Elder Master went on to be reborn as a distinguished Zen Master, while the former young master had by then become the famous Chinese poet Su Tung-P'o (T'ang dynasty). Because of his previous cultivation, Tung-P'o was a mandarin, endowed with intelligence and wisdom. However, being amorous in nature, he was entangled in the conflicting demands of seven wives and concubines. Moreover, with his learning and intelligence, he often challenged the Zen Masters of his day. Only after he was vanquished by his former friend did he return to Zen practice."

The story suggests that delusive thoughts can harm even seasoned practitioners. Merely contemplating and deciding to not have delusive thoughts doesn't work. One has to work hard on meditation to minimize delusive thoughts.

3

MYSTERIOUS EXPERIENCES

Sozan once said to Shie Doja, "Aren't you 'paper clothes the pilgrim'?"

Shie Doja answered, "I am not worthy of being so."

Sozan asked, "What is the thing beneath paper clothes?"

Shie Doja said, "When just a leather garment is put on the body, all things are of their suchness."

Sozan said, "What is the activity beneath paper clothes?"

Shie Doja came near him and died standing up.

Sozan said, "You have expounded the going, but how about the coming?"

Shie Doja suddenly opened his eyes and asked, "How about when a spiritual nature does not borrow a placenta?"

Sozan said, "This is not yet wonderful."

Shie Doja asked, "What is wonderful then?"

Sozan said, "Not-borrowing borrowing."

Shie Doja thereupon said, "Be happy, be well!" and died, sitting.

Sozan made a verse:

The enlightened mind is a perfect and formless body.

Do not believe, unreasonably,

That it is far off or near!

Thoughts of difference becloud the original form.

A mind at variance with itself cannot be in harmony with the way.

When emotion distinguishes phenomena, we fall into materiality.
When intellect judges the manifold, we lose the reality.
If you understand perfectly the meaning of these words,
You are without doubt beyond danger like those of ancient times.

~ Zen, The Quantum Leap from Mind To No-Mind: Osho ~

This anecdote looks much weird. Whenever people encounter such anecdotes, they get rid of the mysterious parts by suggesting the philosophy behind such incidents. People say that such stories are merely a device to impart some wisdom to the next generation. The idea is that since the incident doesn't seem to be natural, they replace it with the suggestive meaning. The same is the case here. How can a man die and then again become alive? So, the philosophers say that this story simply means that one should die deeply so that he doesn't get borne again.

Can a person die and be back to life again? Before we delve into this question, let us quickly understand what the story means.

Sozan is calling Shie Doja 'Paper Clothes – the pilgrim'. All of us are pilgrims. We travel from life to death and perhaps even further without knowing where we have come from and where we are going. And leave aside the talks of coming and going; we don't even know who we are!!!

Such an ignorant person carries a body, but that body is phony because he doesn't know about the owner of the body. Thus, Master Sozan calls it a paper cloth. We all are paper clothes.

But beneath this paper cloth lies the mystery of mysteries. The disciple Shie Doja suggests that what lies within is beyond life and death – beyond coming and going.

When Shie Doja died, the master said that his going was not complete. He could any time take another birth. So, the master again poked the student. The student died again and suggested that now he would not be borne again.

This looks anecdotal because ordinarily, we believe that once someone dies, he can't become alive again. If he becomes alive again, then the doctor thinks that the patient was merely unconscious for some time but was not dead. That's why people explain such stories by considering them as a simile or metaphor. But is it the truth? Can a person die and come back?

Dr Mary Neal is an orthopaedic spine surgeon who drowned while kayaking on a South American river in 1999. She experienced life after death. She went to heaven and had a very soothing experience. After staying dead for around 20 minutes, she came back to life.

Such experiences are called Near Death Experiences (NDEs). Mainstream scientists have a very sick habit of saying that she was lying or was hallucinating. But thousands of such cases around the globe have been reported. It is not possible that all of them were lying, and only one particular scientist is a God of truth!

Hundreds of such cases have been verified by psychologists or, better say, parapsychologists. In most such cases, patients saw the light outside the tunnel, they had a very peaceful experience, and when they returned to life, their whole personalities changed. They became saintly and gentle after returning to life. These remarkable characteristics have been seen in most cases of Near-Death Experiences.

Some people say that it is because of drugs given to the patients, but cases like Mary Neal were not under the influence of any kind of drug. Some people say that it is due to lack of oxygen in the brain this happens. But Dr Bruce Greyson confirms that under the lack of oxygen, people don't have a peaceful experience. NDEs are still a mystery of science!

Fortunately, now scientists can't say that NDEs and reincarnation are hallucination stories, and such phenomena don't happen. Sceptical people can't simply shrug their shoulders and walk away, saying that they don't believe in NDE or reincarnation because now it has become a part of mainstream science. Yes! Prof. Bruce Greyson is Professor Emeritus of Psychiatry and Neurobehavioral Sciences at the University of Virginia. He is the author of 'After: A Doctor Explores What Near-Death Experiences Reveal about Life and Beyond', co-author of 'Irreducible Mind' and co-editor of 'The Handbook of Near-Death Experiences'. He has at least four decades of experience in exploring such cases, and they say that there are still many mysteries which science has not been able to solve yet!

Can people come back to life after death? The argument that people can't come back to life is untenable.

4

PREMONITION

Seoam Sunim died at Bongamsa on the 29th of March 2003, at the age of 87. He had been a monk for sixty-eight years. Before his decease, he assembled about 100 monks and lay people from Taego Seon center and Bongam Monastery and told them, "I have nothing to say. If people ask about my Nirvana poem, tell them, 'There was an old man who lived thus and died thus.' That is my Nirvana poem." He then retired to his room and passed away in a sitting position.

~ http://www.buddhism.org/seoam-honggeun-1917-2003/~

There are many cases of Zen Masters where they knew about their death and died in a sitting meditation position. How can someone know about the future before it happens? If it happens once, it can be called coincidence, but there have been numerous such cases in the past.

Here we are not talking about astrologers. Astrologers don't see the future. They look at the signs in the horoscope, and based on those signs, predict the future. Astrology is considered a pseudo-science, and I wouldn't say much about it here. I myself, being an astrologer, have examined the horoscope of many people and have seen a remarkable connection between one's future and the positioning of the planets at the time of their birth. The set of rules work remarkably for ascendants with similar positioning of planets in their horoscope. However, here we are not talking about astrology. Here we are talking about premonitions.

Consider this scenario: Suppose you come to know that the government has imposed a lockdown for the next week due to COVID or any other dangerous situation. Now looking at the situation, you can predict that you won't go to the school or workplace for the next week. This prediction is based on external signs. Such prediction is not premonition - an actual vision of the future.

How could Zen Masters have known about their future? What does this mean? Does premonition happen? Is the future somehow rooted in the present, which we cannot decode, but some people are? Before abruptly discarding such possibilities, as the mainstream scientists do, let us look at some of the weird cases which have happened in the past century.

Air Marshall Sir Robert Victor Goddard (1897-1987) was flying over an abandoned airfield in Drem, Scotland when he said he encountered a storm. After turbulence almost caused him to crash, Goddard finally managed to regain control of his plane.

But when he looked down at the airfield below him, he saw it was fully functional, with new hangars, strange-looking planes and mechanics in blue uniforms instead of the brown uniforms currently worn in 1935. When Goddard returned from the flight, he told some of his colleagues, but they didn't believe him.

Four years later, the RAF developed and began using the same planes he claimed he'd seen in his 'time travel experience', and they switched their uniforms from brown to blue. Goddard has written about his mysterious experience.

Was it a case of time travel? Or was it a premonition? No one knows.

Katherine Fletcher has written a book "Time Slips: Real Stories of Time Travel". She tells the case of a lady reading a book while sitting on a chair outside her house. Her husband, who had gone outside for some work, came back in his car. The lady tilted her head and saw the car. Her husband came out of the car. She kept on reading her book and turned her head again only to see the car had disappeared. She thought that her husband might have gone away again for some work. After one hour, her husband returned back and stopped the car in the same fashion as she had seen one hour back. When she asked her husband said that he hadn't come to the house one hour ago!

Did that lady actually go to a different time world? Was it a time slip or time travel? Was it a premonition?

There are many such cases of time travel and premonitions. All of them can't be ruled out. It looks tenacious that the Zen Masters could have indeed known about their future.

5

SPIRITS

Zen Master Nan-Ch'uan was meditating in a hut next to a river. One night he heard two ghosts conversing. One of them was rejoicing that his term was coming to an end because the next day someone would be replacing him. The second ghost asked, 'Who will be replacing you?' He replied, 'A man wearing an iron hat.' The master wondered to himself who this person could be. The next day there was heavy rain and the river rose to a higher level. The master looked out of his hut and saw a man about to cross the river. He had covered his head with a wok (a bowl-shaped cooking utensil) for protection against the rain. Immediately, the master knew that this was the man of the iron hat, so he cautioned him saying, 'Don't cross the river today. It's too dangerous.' The man asked, 'Why?' 'Because the water is very deep and running rapidly.' The man listened to the old monk's advice and returned home. You must understand that in Chinese lore, water ghosts are prisoners until another person drowns and takes their place. That night as he was meditating, the master heard the two ghosts again. This time the first ghost was complaining, 'I have been stuck here for so many years, and I thought my chance for freedom had finally come. But now the old monk interfered and messed everything up. I'll show him what I can do.'

Upon hearing this exchange, the master immediately entered samadhi. He saw the demons enter, exit and go around his hut, as if searching for someone. However, thanks to the fact that his mind in samadhi was empty and still, 'not influenced by the environment, no longer tied to mental objects,' the demons could not see him. Discouraged, they finally left.

~ Faith in Mind by Master Sheng Yen ~

Before we try to understand this Zen Story, let's discuss about ghosts. Whenever it comes to ghosts or spirits, people say that they are merely psychological hallucinations. Up to some extent, it is true as well. Nyogen Sangaki tells a famous Zen Story about the subjugation of ghosts in his book Zen Flesh Zen Bones:

'A young wife fell sick and was about to die. "I love you so much," she told her husband, "I do not want to leave you. Do not go from me to any other woman. If you do, I will return as a ghost and cause you endless trouble."

Soon the wife passed away. The husband respected her last wish for the first three months, but then he met another woman and fell in love with her. They became engaged to be married.

Immediately after the engagement a ghost appeared every night to the man, blaming him for not keeping his promise. The ghost was clever too. She told him exactly what has transpired between himself and his new sweetheart. Whenever he gave his fiancée a present, the ghost would describe it in detail. She would even repeat conversations and it so annoyed the man that he could not sleep. Someone advised him to take his problem to a Zen master who lived close to the village. At length, in despair, the poor man went to him for help.

"Your former wife became a ghost and knows everything you do," commented the master. "Whatever you do or say, whatever you give you beloved, she knows. She must be a very wise ghost. Really you should admire such a ghost. The next time she appears, bargain with her. Tell

her that she knows so much you can hide nothing from her, and that if she will answer you one question, you promise to break your engagement and remain single."

"What is the question I must ask her?" inquired the man.

The master replied: "Take a large handful of soybeans and ask her exactly how many beans you hold in your hand. If she cannot tell you, you will know she is only a figment of your imagination and will trouble you no longer."

The next night, when the ghost appeared the man flattered her and told her that she knew everything.

"Indeed," replied the ghost, "and I know you went to see that Zen master today."

"And since you know so much," demanded the man, "tell me how many beans I hold in this hand!"

There was no longer any ghost to answer the question.'

The story is quite clear. The ghost was a mental projection of the husband. Whatever he knew, even the spirit knew. Whatever he didn't know, even the ghost didn't know, and thus he disappeared.

But do ghosts exist? Are all stories of ghosts only imaginary? It doesn't appear so! In this chapter, we shall read some cases which suggest that ghosts do exist:

Case 1: The Mandy Doll

In your childhood, you must have played with dolls. But sometimes you play with dolls, and sometimes dolls start playing with you!! Made in 1910 in Germany, the Mandy doll is one of the most haunted dolls in the world.

Her cracked face is twisted into a sinister-looking half-smile. Her eyes seem to track your movements, and electronics have a habit of acting haywire in Mandy's presence.

She was donated to the Quesnel Museum back in 1991. Her previous owner said that she was plagued by the sound of a baby crying at night. Following the sound to her basement, she found nothing but the breeze blowing through an open window. After finding Mandy in storage in the basement, she donated the creepy vintage porcelain doll to the Quesnel Museum. Mysteriously, the phantom crying stopped once the doll was gone.

Mandy seems content with creeping out visitors and playing tricks on the staff of the museum. Disembodied footsteps have been heard in the museum, staff's lunches go missing, only to be found later stuffed into a drawer. Small items go missing and later turn up in strange places.

Case 2: Haunted Houses

There are hundreds of houses that have been reported to be haunted where more than one person has experienced eerie presences. You can see the list on Wikipedia. Many places are locked, and entrance to such locations are prohibited for ordinary people.

In San Diego, California, there is 1857 built Whaley House. It was the home of Thomas Whaley and his wife, Anna Whaley. Thomas Whaley didn't know that the house he was making was built on a graveyard. A series of paranormal incidents started to happen when the Whaley family started to live there. Their daughter could hear the footsteps of someone walking in the house in the night. Later on, they gave birth to a boy. But when the child was only 18 months old, he died mysteriously. Their daughter Violet Whaley committed suicide by shooting herself. Whoever lived in that house, after the Whaley family, reported having experienced many paranormal incidents. Ultimately the house was turned into a museum.

In 2005, Life Magazine called Whaley House "the most haunted house in America." In 2012, the Whaley House was featured on the

Biography Channel's The Haunting of Regis Philbin. Actually, the actor Regis Philbin didn't believe in ghosts and decided to visit the house. But he encountered many paranormal incidents there and finally commented that there was something going on in that house!

Built-in 1862, Borley Rectory was famous for being "the most haunted house in England." It was built for the parish of Borley and his family. Whoever came to stay there experienced spine-chilling paranormal incidents; some people reported having heard the voice of a laughing child in the night. "Spirit messages" were seen on the walls.

The house was finally demolished in 1944.

Case 3: The Mysterious Overtoun Bridge

In Dumbarton, Scotland, there's an ornate 19th-century bridge called the Overtoun Bridge. But its claim to fame is somewhat sinister. It's nicknamed the "dog suicide bridge."

For decades, dating back to the 1950s, dogs have been jumping from the Gothic-style bridge that crosses a 50-foot (15-meter) ravine. Many news outlets have reported on the bridge, and it's inspired at least one full-length book. Some reports set the number of flying furballs in the hundreds, while others cite fewer. Numbers aside, there's no disputing that a lot of dogs have died at this bridge, and no one knows precisely why.

Sometimes dogs survive the fall but suffer terrible injuries. Others perish soon after their plunges. In at least one instance, a dog allegedly jumped from the bridge, survived, ran up the slope and then jumped off again. But what's inspiring this rash of jumps?

In 2010, the animal behaviourist David Sands stated that dogs commit suicide due to the smell of rats. But rats have been recently seen and have not been abundant in that area since the 1950s. So, his theory is not widely accepted. What is the reason, then? Is the place cursed? Or is there any supernatural activity going on? No one knows!

Case 4: The Cursed Cash

It is widespread in various cultures that ghosts are the carriers of curses. In 2011, Wayne Sabaj, a 51-year-old person, found bags of cash worth around $150,000. He was due to enter into a settlement in court on July 11 that would have split the windfall between him and the neighbour, said his lawyer, Robert Burke.

The neighbour, Delores Johnson, believed that the money was cursed and, therefore, their family had buried them. Delores' daughter had also claimed the money on her parents' behalf, but she died before the case was settled. After winning the case, within few days, Wayne Sabaj died mysteriously. After his death, the money went to Wayne's father.

What I am going to tell you now will chill your spine. Very soon, Wayne's father also died in mysterious circumstances! Was that cash really cursed? No one knows!

Case 5: The Cursed Amethyst

Ever since it was stolen out of India during the Rebellion of 1857, this amethyst has brought its owners nothing but despair and devastation. Known as the Cursed Amethyst or, in a bit of a misnomer, the Delhi Purple Sapphire, the stone now resides in the Vault of the Natural History Museum in London.

The amethyst was stolen out of the Temple of Indra in Kanpur and later on brought to England by Colonel W. Ferris. Yet the beautiful violet stone's sinister nature was soon manifested when he lost just about everything he owned, and his health deteriorated. The same misery happened to his son, who inherited the stone, so he gave it to a friend. But to an eerie twist, the friend also subsequently committed suicide!!

Science finds it difficult to believe in the ghost, not because it can't be seen. Obviously, we can't see the air, but still, we know that air does exist. Science has two serious arguments again soul or ghost or spirit:

First: It goes against the law of conservation of energy. How can a non-physical soul make changes in the world? Making changes in anything involves adding energy into the world.

Second: They don't have any physical attributes, so how can they be differentiated. Understand this! If we have two glasses, one has orange juice, and the other has milk, then they can be separated by looking at the colour of the liquid inside the glass. The soul can also be considered as a glass that contains memories of human beings. But since souls are non-physical, the soul of one person can't be differentiated from other's, and thus it is impossible to distinguish between the ghost of one person and another.

Due to these arguments, science has always been against the soul. But these arguments look pretty specious. The first argument can be refuted by looking at the observation rather than theory. The theory should be modified as per the observation and not vice versa. If there are shreds of evidence that souls or ghosts can make noise or create frightening scenarios, then as per the observation, the law of conservation should be changed. Till Einstein didn't come up with the Special Theory of Relativity, Newton's Law of Motion was considered to be an unchallenged universal law. But it was not. When Einstein's theory was propounded, Newton's Law of motion was changed, and it was suggested that Newton's Laws hold only in an inertial frame. In the non-inertial frame, Newton's Laws of motion were deemed to be incorrect. Similarly, the law of conservation of energy should be accordingly modified to accommodate spirits or souls. The Law of conservation of energy holds as long as any spirit doesn't interfere. By making this change, science, religion and observations all will come to harmony. So, the first objection of science doesn't seem to be a powerful argument against the soul.

Let us examine the second argument. Not having physical characteristics is also not a biggy. From a human's standpoint, of course, there is no physical property of the soul. But from nature's perspective, there might be some. For example: when we look at the seeds of, say, apple, they all appear the same to us. We can't differentiate one seed from another. But nature can. This is why all the seeds don't result in the same number of apples. Nature can distinguish one seed from the other.

So, we see that the existence of the soul can't be refuted satisfactorily by science. Now let's come back to the Zen story which we read at the beginning of this chapter. The ghosts can read your mind and then can cause affliction to you. If you want to be happy, it can create misery in your life. If you want to enjoy life, it can create trouble for you. In the story, the Zen master meditated, making his mind empty of thoughts. Thus, the ghosts couldn't read the master's mind and disappeared!

Zen is not the path of philosophical contemplation. All philosophical discussions take you on an endless journey. You start with a question, and no matter what you answer, each answer gives rise to few more questions. In the end, you will have thousand and one more questions, but the original question will remain unsolved. For thousands of years, philosophers have been discussing whether God exists or not without reaching any conclusion. For thousands of years, philosophers have been discussing whether God takes incarnation or not, and so far, they haven't reached any conclusion.

Zen says that philosophical discussion will lead you to more and more words. Zen suggests we look at the nature of things as they are without any prejudice. This awareness comes through meditation. Meditation is the solution provided by Zen. A person who doesn't meditate and merely keeps on reading these Zen Stories is doing nothing but deceiving himself!

6

TIME TRAVEL

The tengu, 'heavenly-dogs', are considered to be long-nosed goblins or demi-demons; they can also come in a form known as Karasu-tengu that is half man and half crow.

One story of a tengu is as follows. Some boys were tormenting a bird and an old man passed by and saved the bird from dying. As he went on his way a mountain hermit came to him and thanked him, declaring that he was the bird he had saved. The traveller knew that instant that he was talking to a tengu. The tengu offered him supernatural powers in reward but the man said he had no need of them, and his only wish was to see the original Buddha giving a sermon. The tengu said he could transport him through time and space and show him such a thing, but that the man must say nothing and remain silent at all times. The man agreed, and the tengu took him to Vulture Mountain back in the time of the Buddha. There he saw hosts of spirits and demons and holy men listening to the Buddha. Unable to control himself, he cried out in reverence and that instant was transported back to his original position and to face a very angry tengu, who had his wings broken as punishment. The tengu scolded the man and was never seen again.

~ The Dark Side of Japan by Antony Cummins ~

This story looks weird because it talks about time travel where a man went back in Buddha's time. However, he was not able to change the past.

Time Travel is a much-debated topic in the elite world. Einstein's theory of relativity suggests that theoretically, it is possible to travel in a different time and space. Yet, so far, no one has been able to make a time machine.

Merely the theory of time travel leads to paradoxes. Let's discuss two, if not one.

1. **The Grandfather Paradox**
   Suppose a person travels to the past and kills their grandfather before the conception of their father or mother, which prevents the time traveller's existence. Changing the past will then change the future. This is a paradox.
2. **The Knowledge Paradox**

Consider this story: A young man is given a book by an old man. The book contains information about building a time machine, which the young man then sets about building. Years later, as an old man, he travels back in time and gives the same book to his younger self.

This is a bizarre state of affairs. The book is neither created nor destroyed. Furthermore, the knowledge contained in the book comes from nowhere, without anybody expending any effort to acquire it.

Some people resolve this problem by saying that time travellers will have some pretty unusual constraints. He would not be able to change it. But one school of thought says that he can if he goes to a parallel universe. The concept of a parallel universe was brought to fix such paradoxes!

There have been some people like John Titor and Noah who have claimed to be time travellers, but they have been debunked by experts. On Wikipedia, there is a page called 'Time travel claims and urban legends'. This page debunks the claims of time travel.

Yet, there are few cases that have intrigued the experts. Let me share a couple with you.

The Taured Mystery

It was July 1954 when a smartly dressed man arrived at Haneda Airport in Tokyo, Japan. Much like other passengers, he makes his way to customs. But whatever happened from this point onwards have left all puzzled and concerned. When questioned by the customs officers, the mysterious passenger said he was from Taured, also referred to as Taured Mystery. The mystery man claimed that it was the third time he was visiting Japan from his country. But, to the surprise of officers, they couldn't find any country named Taured. The primary language of the man, described as Caucasian looking with a beard, was French. However, he was purportedly speaking Japanese and many other languages as well. Officers were perplexed because they had never heard about any such country. The passport of the man was issued by, of course, the Taured. The passport looked authentic, but the place was not recognized.

Location of Taured

The man was then given a map and asked to point out his country. He immediately man pointed to the area occupied by the Principality of Andorra. Andorra is at the border of France and Spain. The man said that his country has been in existence for 1000 years and was a little puzzled why his country was called Andorra on the map. The man argued with the customs officers for long and refused to give in.

Later on, he was asked to stay in a hotel in very tight security in order to conduct further interrogation. To ensure that the mystery man didn't escape, two guards were placed on the door. It must be mentioned that the hotel room in which he was staying only had one entry and exit point. But to everyone's surprise, the man vanished the following day. Not only that, but all his personal documents had also disappeared. A search was launched to find the man but in vain. The thing that was troubling investigating officers was that he was put up in a room high up in the multi-storey hotel building with no balcony.

Some people argued that the mystery man was indeed from Taured, but the country happens to be in another universe and somehow passed through a parallel dimension and ended up at Haneda Airport. Another theory is that the mystery man was a time traveller and had mistakenly landed at the airport. Above all this, there are people who claim that it's just an elaborate internet hoax.

The Lost Time

In the 1970s, a bizarre situation is said to have occurred involving a (now defunct) National Airlines 727 during its approach to Miami International Airport. All was normal as the plane and its passengers drew closer to MIA – until the flight captain received a message to land in an emergency. There was no apparent problem of weather or any other kind. So, the pilot, as well as the passengers, got frustrated due to the emergency landing.

When the annoyed pilot checked with the control tower people, he came to know that the plane completely vanished from radar for 10 minutes, and all radio communications ceased. While the radar could detect other planes, the above-mentioned plane was not being detected on the radar. This might appear to be a technical fault, the astute readers might think. But the pilot's watch, the cockpit's watch, and the passengers' watch all showed 9:20 while it was 9:30. It appears that for 10 minutes, either the time ceased, or they went to another parallel universe!

These cases suggest that the possibility of time travel isn't too far-fetched!

7

LA CHAQUIRA

"At that time Sessen Doji (a previous incarnation of Buddha Shakyamuni) had mastered the Brahman and other non-Buddhist teachings but had not yet heard of Buddhism. The god Indra decided to test his resolve. He appeared before Sessen Doji in the form of a hungry demon and recited half a verse from a Buddhist teaching: 'All is changeable, nothing is constant. This is the law of Birth and Death.' Hearing this, Sessen Doji begged the demon to tell him the second half. The demon agreed but demanded his flesh and blood in payment. Sessen Doji gladly consented, and the demon taught him the latter half of the verse: 'Extinguishing the cycle of Birth and Death, one enters the joy of Nirvana.' Sessen Doji scrawled this teaching on the rocks and trees for the sake of others who might pass by, and then jumped from a tall tree into the demon's mouth. Just at that moment the Demon changed back into the god Indra and caught him before he fell. He praised Sessen Doji's willingness to give his life for the Dharma and predicted that he would certainly attain Buddhahood."

~ The Parinirvana Sutra ~

La Chaquira is an ancient site in Colombia. It has a huge rock with this weird carving as shown in the pic. It shows a man, with big eyes and mysterious smile, pointing up towards the sky. No one knows who built it and why.

This is not the only figure like that. There is another mysterious site in Peru where miles long Nazca Lines are drawn. It can be seen only from the sky. One of those carvings is the El Astronauta, the Astronaut who is also pointing towards the sky.

Archaeologists don't know why it is called Chaquira, but people living nearby say that he is the God of the sky and lightning or thunderstorms. This is interesting because there is a Mayan God called Chac, who is also the God of thunder and lightning.

(Image of La Chaquira, taken from Wikipedia)

(Image of El Astronauta Nazca Lines, taken from Wikipedia)

In Hindu and Buddhist mythology, Indra is the king of Devloka, which is another planet. Surprisingly, another name of Indra is Shakra or Shaka. Is La Chaquira a Colombian form of Shakra? Did an alien build this? Did Indra come to earth? No one knows! But one thing is sure that whoever wrote those scriptures didn't come up with such stories out of thin air!

8 |

LEVITATION

Sometimes tengu steal people and return them in a demented state; this is referred to as tengu-kakushi or being 'hidden by a Tengu'. One example of this is Kiuchi, a samurai who went missing; his fellows came upon his equipment strewn around and, in the end, found him on a temple roof, at which point he told his story. He said that he had met with a black-robed monk and a larger man with a red face. They had told him that he must climb onto the temple roof, and when he refused, they broke his sword and scabbard and carried him to the roof. There they made him sit on a tray, and through magic they made the tray float; it took him through the skies to many regions across the land. After ten days of this, Kiuchi prayed to Buddha. The tray then landed on a mountain, but the mountain turned into the roof of the temple where he had begun.

~ The Dark Side of Japan by Antony Cummins ~

This story looks like a legend because it talks about the floating of a tray in the air through some kind of magic.

In the beginning, we talked about few massive monolithic monuments, made of rocks weighing in tons, in various corners of the globe. As per the mainstream archaeologists, our ancestors carried those voluminous heavy rocks using bamboos and ropes. This doesn't seem to be sensible.

Science has recently been able to build anti-gravity systems that can help any object to levitate in the air. Some extra-terrestrial theorists have given a theory that our ancestors used to move the heavy rocks using a similar anti-gravity technique or through some acoustic levitation technique or mantra. They also suggest that aliens or extra-terrestrials taught the techniques to human beings.

Whatever be the case, levitation isn't an impossible phenomenon. Many ancient scriptures point towards such stories. In Ramayana, there is the story of the Monkey God Hanumana, who could fly in the sky and cross the ocean. In the Buddhist Tripitaka scriptures, there is a story when they arrived at a bank to fight with each other Buddha levitated to the sky and stopped them from fighting. Here is the story is taken from 'The Great Chronicle of Buddhas' by Ven. Mingun Sayadaw:

'There was a small river by the name of Rohini between Kapilavatthu and Koliya. The two kingdoms took turns, in perfect harmony, to water their respective arable lands by controlling the flow of the channel with a single dam.

The level of the water in the channel was at its lowest in the month of Jetthamasa and the crops usually withered. The farmers of the two countries called a meeting to discuss the matter of sharing the water in the channel.

At the meeting the farmers of Koliya said:

"Friends, if the small amount of water in the reservoir were to be divided and shared by both of us, none of us would receive sufficient amount to water our fields. One more flood of water would suffice to bring maturity to our crops. We request you therefore to let us make use of this small amount of water." Farmers of Kapilavatthu had their say also in this manner:

"Friends, we can't go from door to door of your houses carrying baskets and our purses filled with gold, silver and precious jewels in search of paddy, in a dejected manner, while you all sat down with your minds at ease having filled your granaries with paddy to their full capacities. Our early crops, too, are about to mature and need watering in like manner."

Heated arguments ensued, one side saying 'we are not going to yield', the other side retorting in the same words. Exchange of words eventually led to blows, a farmer on one side starting to attack a farmer from the other side and the latter retaliating in a like manner. The affray that started between the farmers on both sides ultimately grew into hostilities (like a small bush fire which grows fierce and finally burns down a palatial mansion) to the extent of decrying the royal clans on both sides.

The Koliyan farmers began the quarrel:

"You have threatened us by placing your reliance on the royal clan of Kapilavatthu. These Kapilavatthu royal clan you depend upon behave like common dogs and jackals of the forest making their own sisters their wives. What harm can their elephants, horses and armours can do to us?"

The Kapilavatthu farmers retaliated in no less acrimonious tone:

"You threatened us by relying on your little lepers inflicted with horrible leprosy. The Koliya descendents on whom you lean for support are themselves in a miserable plight ever since they were banished from the city and lived like animals in the hollow of Kola trees. What harm can their elephants, horses and armours can do to us?"

The farmers returned to their respective cities and reported the matter to the Ministers of Agriculture, who in turn, brought the state of affairs to the notice of their chiefs.

Consequently, the Sakyans of Kapilavatthu prepared to wage war on Koliyas and came out of the city, shouting the war cry: "The hus-

bands of their own sisters will demonstrate their feat of arms." The ri-
val royalties on the side of Koliyas also prepared for war and came out,
their war cry being: "Those taking shelters in the hollows of Kola trees
will display their feat of arms."

At that time, the Buddha was still residing in the Jetavana
monastery of Savatthi. On the very day on which the two rival commu-
nities of Kapilavatthu and Koliya were all prepared to go to the battle-
field, He surveyed the world early at dawn and perceived that a bloody
battle was imminent between the two opposing sides that very evening.
He further perceived that He would be able to avert the war by going to
the scene of hostilities and expounding them about the true religion."

Having perceived thus, the Buddha decided to go to the place of
hostilities and save the warring kinsmen from mutual destruction.
He went early for the usual round of receiving alms-food and stayed
the whole day in the Scented Chamber. Towards evening, He left the
Chamber, carrying the big robe and alms bowl himself, for the scene of
strife all alone, without informing anyone. On arrival at the spot, He
sat cross-legged in the sky in the middle of the rival groups, and caused
dark-blue rays to be emitted from His hair so that darkness prevailed
all over, although the sun had not yet set. This was meant to cause con-
trition in the heart of the warring factions.

While all the people were greatly frightened by the strange phe-
nomenon, the Buddha, sending out six-coloured rays from His body,
manifested Himself to them.

Peace

When members of the Sakyan clan saw the Buddha, they began to
contemplate thus: "The Buddha of our own blood has come, perhaps
He has full knowledge of our strife." They discussed among themselves
and decided: "It is not right and proper for us to let our weapons fall
upon the bodies of others in the presence of the Buddha; let Koliyans kill
us or take us captives, should they desire to do so." By mutual consent

they abandoned all their weapons and sat down respectfully making homage to the Buddha.

The Koliyans also arrived at the same decision among themselves. They too abandoned their weapons and sat down paying obeisance to the Buddha who then descended from the sky and sat on a reserved seat on the delightful sandy plain, with all the grace and glory of a Buddha. Buddha then taught them to live with peace and harmony.'

These stories suggest that our ancients were prudent and had some technologies of levitating, which we have somehow lost.

9

WHOOSH...

Kakua visited China and accepted the true teaching. He did not travel while he was there. Meditating constantly, he lived on a remote part of a mountain. Whenever people found him and asked him to preach, he would say a few words and then move to another part of the mountain where he could be found less easily.

The emperor heard about Kakua when he returned to Japan and asked him to preach Zen for his edification and that of his subjects.

Kakua stood before the emperor in silence. He then produced a flute from the folds of his robe and blew one short note. Bowing politely, he disappeared.

After Kakua visited the emperor, he disappeared, and no one knew what became of him. He was the first Japanese to study Zen in China, but since he showed nothing of it, save one note, he is not remembered for having brought Zen into his country.

~ Zen Flesh Zen Bones by Paul Reps & Nyogen Senzaki ~

The Truth can't be given to someone. If it could be given, then once Buddha was enlightened, he could have given to the whole world, and the whole world would have become enlightened. But it doesn't happen like that. The message of the story is clear. But one thing remains surprising. How did Kakua disappear? Can a person disappear?

In mythological stories, there are numerous accounts of God who used to come from heaven and disappear. But can a human being disappear too?

Let me tell you the mysterious case of Ambrose Bierce. This is one of the most famous mysteries of any author. Ambrose Bierce was born in 1841 in the United States. He was a famous science fiction writer. One of his most famous books is "The Difficulty of Crossing a Field". In this story, a character crosses a field and suddenly disappears without leaving any trace. This story was published in 1888.

In October 1913, Ambrose left Washington D.C. for a tour of his old Civil War battlefields. On December 26, 1913, he wrote a letter to a close friend Blanche Partington. After closing this letter by saying, "As to me, I leave here tomorrow for an unknown destination," he vanished without a trace.

Which unknown destination was he talking about? Did he go with aliens? Despite an abundance of theories, Bierce's ultimate fate remains a mystery.

There is another case of Cornelio Closa. In September 1951, when he was 13 years old, he was walking home with his classmate Rudolfo from Zamora Elementary School in Manila, Philippines. It was a clear day, and there were no signs of oddities. But suddenly, Cornelio saw a fairy kind of girl who was not visible to his classmate Rudolfo. And within few moments, Cornelio disappeared right in front of Rudolfo. Later on, Cornelio appeared again unharmed.

You might say that Rudolfo was hallucinating. But this was not the end of the story. This was only the beginning of a series of paranormal phenomena. Cornelio kept on disappearing time and again in front of his family members and kept on appearing abruptly in another place, often scaring eyewitnesses!

Another mysterious incident took place in China during the 1930s. A war between Japan and China was going on. One night, the commander of a battalion of around 3 thousand soldiers in Nanking went to bed as normal after checking his troops. The next morning, he woke up with a piece of disturbing news. All the 3000 soldiers had disappeared without leaving a trace. Their clothes and weapons were there, but their bodies vanished. There were no signs of abduction or massacre! The mystery remains unsolved to date.

It appears that human beings can disappear. How can they disappear is a mystery unsolved!

Let's close this chapter with another wonderful story from Zen Antics by Thomas Cleary:

'*Fūgai met more than ten Zen teachers, but his own mind was so sharp and free that no one could equal him. Finally, he met the redoubtable Genrō the Wolf and attained great enlightenment at a single saying of the great Zen master. After he mastered the inner teachings, Fūgai left Genrō and disappeared into anonymity to mature his spiritual development.*'

10

ZENSATIONAL MATHS

Someone asked, "What is the way beyond (sufferings)?"
Zen Master Yunmen said, "Nine times nine is eighty-one."

~ Records of Yunmen (Translated by Urs App) ~

I hope this story is not too complicated to understand. The master means to say, 'You have not even begun learning to calculate and are already talking of such big numbers?"

The numbers have intrigued human beings for aeons. Numbers have a lot of significance in our life. We can't imagine a progressive society without numbers. There is a tribe in Brazil called Piraha. They have words for one, two and many. They don't have words for three, four and higher numbers. Scientists have found that not having higher numbers limits the tribe's concept of numbers. In an experiment, they discovered that the Piraha could copy patterns of one, two, or three objects but made significant errors when asked to deal with four or higher numbers of things. Some philosophers consider this to be the most substantial evidence yet for linguistic determinism. This theory suggests that understanding is ring-fenced by language, and at least in some areas, we can't think about things we don't have words for!

It is said that around two thousand and five hundred years ago, the Greek philosopher and mathematician Pythagoras had set up a cult where people believed that the mystery of the world is hidden in numbers. He is attributed to be the founder of the Pythagoras theorem, which says that a right-angled triangle having sides a, b and c, with c as a hypotenuse follows the rule: a squared + b squared = c squared. For example, a right-angled triangle with sides 3, 4 and 5 (hypotenuse) follows 3 squared + 4 squared = 9 + 16 = 25 = 5 squared.

There are few numbers which are indeed having special features. For example, Nine. Nine is the biggest digit in the decimal system. The numbers after nine are numbers that reuse digits from 0 to 9. Nine has a special property. Multiply any number by nine. Whatever is the output, sum up all the digits of that number. If the sum is of two or more digits, then keep on adding the digits again and again until you get a single-digit number. That number turns out to be nine. For example, multiple 65 with 9, and you will get 585. If you sum up the digits 5, 8 and 5 you get 18. If you sum up 1 and 8, you finally get 9.

It is a weird coincidence that this is my ninth book. Though I started to write another book much earlier than even when I hadn't thought about such a book on mystery, somehow, I was not able to complete that other book. Adding to this coincidence, this chapter is the ninth chapter of the book!

There is a number called mysterious number. It is 6174. Surprisingly, if you go on adding all the digits of this number, you again get 9!

Anyway, you would ask what the mystery is behind 6174. In 1949 the mathematician D. R. Kaprekar from India devised a process. That process I named Kaprekar's operation. First of all, choose a four-digit number where the digits are not all the same. For example: don't choose 9999 because all the digits are some. For understanding purposes, let's take the number 1392. Now use the four digits of the number to make the biggest number and smallest number. In our case, we have 1,3,9 and 2. The biggest number which can be formed using these digits is 9321, and the smallest number is 1239. Subtract the small one from the large one and keep on repeating this process.

Let's try it out.

9321 - 1239 = 8082

Now we have 8082. Using these four digits 8,0,8 and 2, the largest number that can be formed is 8820, and the smallest one is 0228. Let's repeat the same operation.

9321 - 1239 = 8082

8820 - 0288 = 8532

8532 – 2358 = 6174

7641 – 1467 = 6174

As you can see, after getting 6174, the process comes to an end. You keep on getting 6174.

No matter which four digits number you take, you will end up getting 6174 when you perform this operation.

There is another mysterious number, 666. It is called the antichrist number or devil's number. A long time ago, when the church was in power, this number was banned. You won't be surprised to see that if you sum the digits of this number, you get 18 and when you sum up 1 and 8, you again end up with 9!

Many religions depend heavily on number symbolism and use special numerical methods for discovering or concealing secrets. In the early years of Christianity, the Romans used the Magic Square of the Sun as a talisman. In this magic square of six-by-six numbers, the numbers 1 to 36 are arranged so that the rows, columns and diagonals add up to 111. The sum of all numbers from 1 to 36 is 666, which, as I said, was considered to be Devil's number. The church banned the possession of the magic square, too, because, in Christianity, 666 is Devil's number. Possession of the magic square became punishable by death.

There is a Belephegor's Prime number. This number is a palindromic prime number. A palindrome is something that reads the same from either side for example, Ada. Whether you read it from left to right or right to left, it reads the same. And a prime number is divisible either by one or by itself. It is not divisible by any other number. Coming back to our Belphegor's prime, it is of the following form:

1<13 Zeroes>666<13 Zeroes>1

You can see the devil's number hidden there, and a long time ago, it was considered to be bringing misfortune!

You might have heard about the imaginary number. The square root of 4 is two, and the square root of 1 is 1. Why? Because when you multiply two by 2, you get 4. When you multiply one by 1, you get 1. Thus 2 is the square root of 4, and 1 is the square root of 1. But what about the square root of MINUS 1. Well, it is not real, and thus a new notation called 'i' was initiated to notify such a number. But can you guess what will be i to the power i, i.e. i^i? Surprisingly it is not imaginary. It turns out to be around 0.207, a real number!

Another interesting number is pi. Pi signifies the ratio of circumference to the diameter of a circle. It is always the same and denoted by pi. It is a constant and roughly equals 22/7 = 3.142857142.... Noting the first three digits, 3 and 1 and 4, many people celebrate pi day on the 14 of March every year!

In 2008, a 150-diameter crop circle suddenly appeared by Barbury Castle near the English village of Wroughton. No one knew who made it. It appeared overnight. Researchers and conspiracy theorists were puzzled over its origin and meaning. An astrophysicist found a weird coincidence that the image was a code representing the first digits of pi!

There is an interesting story behind the pizza. Do you know why it is called pizza? Suppose you take a cylinder of radius z and height a. What will be its volume? The area of the circle will be pi times z times z. When the area of the circle is multiplied by the height of the cylinder, it will come out to be pi * z * z * a and will give us the volume of the cylinder. And therefore, it is called pizza!

In Paola, Malta, there is the Hypogeum of Hal Saflieni. It is a Neolithic structure hewn out of rock, three storeys high. It dated more than five thousand years old and was discovered accidentally in 1902 when workers were cutting cisterns for new housing development. Surprisingly, in the Hypogeum, there is an oracle room that has the property of producing a powerful acoustic resonance from any vocalization made inside it. While other chambers are ordinary, this particular chamber only has the property that a male voice tuned to frequency 70Hz or 114Hz can stimulate the resonance phenomenon throughout the Hypogeum! (Ref: 'Archaeoacoustic Analysis of the Hal Saflieni Hypogeum in Malta' by Prof.agg. Paolo Debertolis and Dr. Fernando Augusto Coimbra, Centro Português de Geohistóiria e Pré-História, Lisboa, Portugal.) Those who know about resonance might be knowing that resonance is taught in the Engineering curriculum, and to understand them, one needs to have advanced knowledge of Mathematics, specially Trigonometry. Who built it? Why did he build it? What was the purpose of such a structure? These questions remain unanswered, but one thing is sure that whoever made it had advanced knowledge of Mathematics. How could he have possessed such knowledge five thousand years ago is another mystery which remains unsolved!

We know that the ancient Egyptian civilization is one of the oldest cultures in human history. Ancient Egyptians are well-known for pioneering all the significant fields of art, science, medicine and mathematics. They used to tell the story of science through mythology. They mastered the integration of science, anatomy and mythology into artistic symbols and figures. The symbol of the Eye of Horus was one of the most significant mysterious mythology used as a sign of prosperity and protection. This symbol has an astonishing connection between neuroanatomical structure and function. Artistically, the Eye is comprised of six different parts. From the mythological standpoint, each part of the Eye is considered to be an individual symbol. Additionally, parts of the Eye represent terms in the series 1/2, 1/4, 1/8, 1/16, and 1/32; when this image is superimposed upon a sagittal image of the human brain, each part appears corresponds to the anatomic location of a particular human sensorium.

The portal cureus.com gives a remarkable insight into the Eye of Horus. Following is extract from the website:

'The Eye of Horus mythology begins with the story of Osiris. This story is the most recognized mythology in ancient Egypt. It illustrates the eternal fight between the virtuous, the sinful, and the punishment. Osiris was the oldest son of the God of the Earth, Geb, and the Goddess of the Sky, Nut, and was known as the God of the Underworld but, more appropriately, as the God of Transition, Resurrection, and Regeneration. Osiris had three siblings: Isis, Set, and Nephthys. Osiris married his sister, Isis, as was the timely Royal custom, and had a son named Horus. The myth started when Set, Osiris' brother, murdered Osiris to claim the throne, which caused disorder and chaos in ancient Egypt. Set's brutality did not stop at killing Osiris, and he proceeded to cut Osiris' body into 14 parts that were distributed across ancient Egypt. According to the ancient Egyptian traditions, in order for a royal's spirit to cross to the underworld, the body needed to be appropriately embalmed and buried in the royal tombs. This proper burial

allowed the body to pass through the underworld gates and be judged according to their deeds.

Isis traveled with Horus in search of Osiris's body parts. Isis also recruited the help of her sister, Nephthys, and Nephthys' son, Anubis. Anubis was the son of Nephthys and Osiris, and it is said that Nephthys wickedly assumed the shape of Isis to seduce Osiris and conceive Anubis. Isis, Nephthys, Anubis, and Horus were able to find 13 parts of Osiris. The spirit of Osiris was then able to pass to Amenti, the underworld, and rule the dead. When Horus killed Set in the large battle near Edfu, he proclaimed his kingdom, restoring the order to Egypt.

The ancient Egyptians used this legendary fight as a metaphor of the battle between good and evil, order and chaos. Afterward, Horus was idolized by the ancient Egyptians in the form of the Eye of Horus, which was considered as a symbol of prosperity and protection.

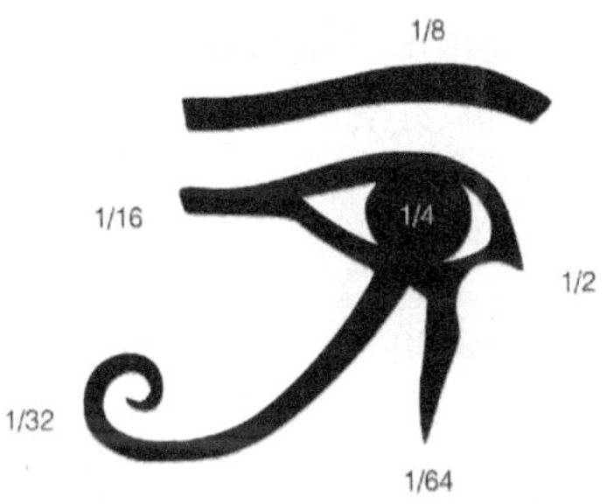

The Eye of Horus fragments were organized together to form the whole Eye, similar to the myth, and these fragments were given a series of numerical values with a numerator of one and dominators to the powers of two: 1/2, 1/4, 1/8, 1/16, 1/32, and 1/64. Some historians suggested that each part of the eye represents one of the six senses: smell, sight, thought, hearing, taste, and touch. Surprisingly, if we superimposed these suggested parts over the mid-sagittal image of the

human brain, each component corresponds to portions of human neu-roanatomical features.

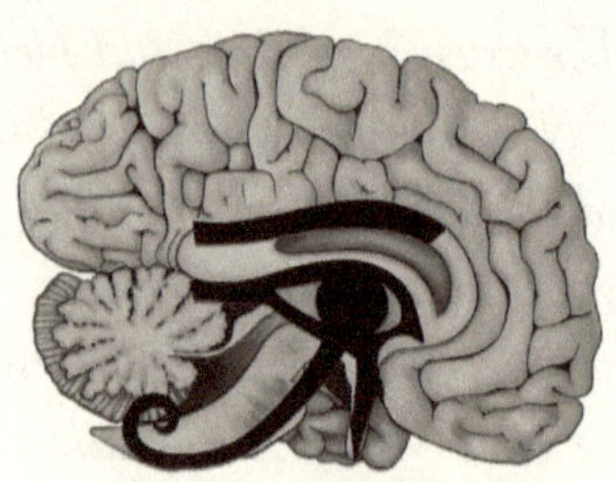

This figure shows the different parts of the Eye of Horus fitting the anatomical structures that carry special brain function depicted by the fractions.'

(Reference: Refaey K, Quinones G C, Clifton W, et al. (May 23, 2019) The Eye of Horus: The Connection Between Art, Medicine, and Mythology in Ancient Egypt. Cureus 11(5): e4731. doi:10.7759/cureus.4731)

Those who want to see how those fractions are connected with human sensorium should check the cureus.com website. But, the ancient Egyptians were pretty experts in various fields.

All these interesting pieces of stuff about maths, mainstream scientists suggest, were identified in the past few centuries. But recently, a new branch of science has been initiated called Pyramidology. The studies of pyramidologists indicate that those who built the pyramids had advanced knowledge of mathematics. They already knew about pi, the golden ratio and other advanced mathematical concepts.

How is it possible? Where did they get such information from? Some people say that advanced aliens came from outer space and gave that knowledge to human beings. But there is no consensus among experts regarding this question!

11

SLEEPLESS

Zen teacher Shouxun of Buddha Lamp Temple was a disciple of Fojian. He went to follow the congregation into the hall to ask for instruction, but it was crowded and there was no room for him. He lamented, "If I do not get total realization in this life, I swear never to spread out my coverlet to sleep."

From then on, he stood there leaning against a pillar for forty-nine days, as if mourning for his dead mother, until he attained great enlightenment.

~ Meditating with Koans by Thomas Cleary ~

Such stories appear to be symbolic to mainstream people because they think that a man can't stay awake for 49 days. They say that such stories merely convey the fact that one needs to work hard on meditation in order to reap its benefits. It is just like going to the gym. You need to go regularly to the gym in order to maintain a healthy body. Going to the gym intermittently in an undisciplined fashion is not going to help. So, they conclude that this story is merely symbolic because one can't stay awake for 49 days. Ordinarily, they are right. However, our universe is more mysterious than ordinary people think.

Have you heard about Mr Thai Ngoc, the sleepless guy? He was born in 1942. In 1973 he came down with a fever. His fever was gone soon, but after that, he hasn't been able to sleep a wink. Yes, he has been awake since then! He assures that a lack of sleep does not affect him physically, boasting of being able to carry two 110 lbs sacks of rice over 2 miles to his house every day!

The case of Thai Ngoc suggests that it is possible to stay awake for longer times. The process is not known yet, but it is not impossible!

In Zen Circles, there is a famous story of Bodhidharma who kept on staring at wall for nine years. In the book 'Records of the Transmissio of the Lamp' (Vol 5, translated by Randolph S. Whitfield), there is a wonderful anecdote in this regard:

A monk asked Chan master Anyong of Mount Shuangquan, 'What is the meaning of Bodhidharma gazing at a wall for nine years?'

'Couldn't sleep,' came the reply!

12

DREAMS

Once, Nansen decided to visit a village, but was very surprised to find that preparations had been made to welcome him.

Nansen said to the village head, "It has been my custom never to let anyone know beforehand about where I am journeying to. How could you know that I was coming to visit your village today?"

The village head replied, "Last night, in a dream, the God of the soil-shrine reported to me that you would come to visit today."

Nansen replied, "This shows how weak and shallow my spiritual life is that it can be foreseen by visions!"

~ Faith in Mind by Sheng Yen ~

This story appears to be a myth because, ordinarily, dreams are not actual incidents. People see various weird kinds of things in dreams. A dream coming true is merely considered to be a coincidence.

Also, ordinary people merely see a pearl of wisdom hidden behind the story. Society wants you to become as mechanical as possible. Society is not full of Buddhas. Society is full of mediocre men. They are not awake. They are asleep. Only an asleep man can allow negativities to sink in their mind. An awake man will live with awareness. Just look within your heart, and you will see all kinds of frustrations, waves of anger, lust and defilements hiding there. A Buddha lives with awareness, and thus, his heart lacks defilements.

These asleep people had made a mechanical world around them. People live in various kinds of unscientific beliefs. If you become vigilant and start questioning them, they will become angry because an asleep person doesn't want to wake up. The more awake you become, the more unpredictable you become. Because an awake person takes decision spontaneously based on the current situation. Ordinary people make decisions based on the conditioning of society and their religions. They don't live in the present. Someone lacks 5000 years ago because their scriptures were written five thousand years ago. Someone is living in 1400 years old world because his religion was established 1400 years ago. An awake person lives in the moment and thus is unpredictable because he doesn't live according to the books. He lives according to his wisdom and the demand of the present situation.

Only an asleep person doesn't see anything wrong with the foundations of society, which are not based on evidence; instead, they are based on a deep-seated need to believe. The faith systems followed by society can be said just only when most of the people born in the society would have become Jesus or Buddha or Lao Tzu. Since the case is totally opposite, an awake person will question the faith systems. Society doesn't like such an awake person because it hurts to accept that whatever they believe has no foundation of truth. Therefore, many times, when such an awake person dwells on the earth, society tries to crucify him. This is why Jesus was crucified, and Socrates was poisoned! It is unfortunate that asleep people are in majority and awakened people are very few.

In the story, Master Nansen realized that he was very predictable, and thus he decided to work hard on his Zen practices so that he could become more current. This is the crux of the Zen Story.

Understanding the moral of the story is easy but believing the facticity of the story is a bit difficult because it suggests that dreams can make predictions. Let us recheck our belief after reading this case:

On 15th September 1981, Barbara Garwell had a dream involving the shooting of an important Middle Eastern man at a stadium. She also saw a single row of seated men, all wearing dark pin-striped suits, in the stadium. The men had 'coffee-coloured skin. She knew her premonition would take 21 days to show effect, and on 6th October, President Anwar Sadat of Egypt was murdered at a mass commemoration.

You might say that this was merely a coincidence. But similar incidents happened again and again, and there are written documents of at least three such incidents. (Journal of the Society for Psychical Research: https://www.keithhearne.com/wp-content/uploads/2010/06/THREE-PREMONITIONS.pdf) She has also written a book "Dreams That Come True: A Medium's Predictions from the Past and Visions of the Future" which is available on Amazon. It is hard to believe that every time coincidences were happening.

There are many cases of premonitions where someone dreamt something, and it really happened exactly as per their dream. So, sometimes dreams can predict the future and people have to live with this fact!

Ancient scriptures have always been talking about such dreams. For example: in Ramayana, there is a story that Bharata, the younger brother of Rama, goes to bring his elder brother Rama, who was in exile, back home. One night, Sita, Rama's wife, saw in the dream that Bharat is going to come along with other family members, and it indeed happens the next day.

In the same scripture, Ramayana, one of the demon lady Trijata, sees in the dream that a monkey is going to burn the kingdom of Lanka, and it indeed happened the next day!

All these stories suggest that sometimes people see dreams which appear to be different from ordinary dreams. People see a dream and forget it. But there are some dreams which keep on haunting people as if it is really going to happen, and such dreams sometimes come true. How it happens and why it happens is not clear, but it does happen.

13

THE MOON MYSTERY

It was a bright moonlit night, and three friends were sitting under the stars and talking about this and that. They had all studied with the same teacher and had many memories to share.

The night went on, the talk went on, until it seemed they had run out of things to say so they sat in companionable silence for a while.

Suddenly one of them pointed to a basin of water that sat at their feet, in which the reflection of the great golden moon could be seen, apparently floating gently on the surface. 'When the water is clear,' he said, 'the moon comes out.'

They all sat there for a few moments, enjoying the moon up above them and the moon below them. Then one of them said, 'When the water is clear the moon does not come out.'

They all laughed over this and then the one who had not spoken suddenly kicked the water basin over, which made them all laugh the harder.

~ The Spirit of Zen by Sam van Schaik ~

Hegel, the philosopher, has talked about dialectics. He says that for every thesis, there is an antithesis. A synthesis tries to bridge the gap. Zen's approach to life is totally different. It doesn't ask you to be indulged in the philosophical discussion because it never comes to an end. Zen simply kicks the water basin and asks you to enjoy life as it is.

Anyway, this story is clear, but I would like to tell a very mysterious thing about the Moon. You might have thought a lot about the origin of Earth. But do you know, scientists still don't know how the Moon was formed!

Capture theory suggests that the Moon was a wandering body (like an asteroid) that formed elsewhere in the solar system and was captured by Earth's gravity as it passed nearby. In contrast, accretion theory suggested that the Moon was created along with Earth at its formation. Finally, according to the fission scenario, Earth had been spinning so fast that some material broke away and began to orbit the planet.

What is most widely accepted today is the giant-impact theory. It proposes that the Moon formed during a collision between the Earth and another small planet, about the size of Mars. The debris from this impact collected in orbit around Earth to form the Moon.

14

PSYCHIC READING

In the Dispensation of Gautama Buddha Khema was born in a princely family at Sagala by the name of Khema. The colour of her complexion was that of gold. She was exceptionally beautiful. She married King Bimbisara of Kosala, who was an enthusiastic supporter of the Buddha. She was reluctant however, to visit the Buddha for fear that the Blessed One would moralise on the fleeing nature of beauty.

Every time she visited the monastery, she dodged meeting the Buddha. One day the king got his men to take her to the Buddha without her suspecting a meeting had been arranged. On her arrival, the Buddha read her mind and created a phantom of unsurpassing beauty to attend on Him. The beauty of the phantom overwhelmed Khema. While she was thus engaged, she felt that beauty could only beguile. The Buddha made the figure to go through youth, middle age, and old age and thereafter to extreme old age devoid of everything worthwhile. Beauty thus gave way to hideousness. It was a graphic picture. Khema understood the meaning and felt what was in store for her: Anicca, Dukkha and Anatta in other words transiency, sorrow and not-self.

To a mind thus prepared the Buddha taught. The seeds fell on good ground. She entered the stream of sainthood (sotapanna).

~ Adapted from Buddhanet.net and 'The Stories about the Foremost Elder Nuns' translated by Anandajoti Bhikkhu ~

This profound story orients us towards the eternal truth of life – impermanence. Now, there are two weird pieces of stuff here: one about creating an illusory phantom of a beautiful lady and the other reading the mind of Khema.

The first power can be explained by 3-D projections, which science has developed. And the second one about reading the mind too has official proof. In the United States, now the police have started to take help from Psychics who can read other people's minds or can have other psychic powers like telepathy. They can touch any object and tell about the whereabouts of anyone who has used that object. Such psychics have helped to solve a lot of criminal cases. There is a page about Psychic Detectives on Wikipedia, which you might see to investigate further.

I would like to finish this chapter with an interesting Taoist story, which talks about how the master could read his disciple's mind and know about his intentions. What follows here is the story called 'The Archer' by Nakashima Ton:

Chi Ch'ang aspired to be the greatest archer in the world, so he became the pupil of Wei Fei.

First Wei Fei ordered him to learn not to blink. Chi Ch'ang crept under his wife's loom and lay there on his back staring without blinking at the treadle as it rushed up and down directly before his eyes. After two years he had reached the point of not blinking even if one of his eyelashes was caught in the treadle.

"To know how not to blink is only the first step," said Wei Fei, "next you must learn to look. Practise looking at things, and if the time comes when what is minute seems conspicuous, and what is small seems huge, visit me once more."

Chi Ch'ang searched for a tiny insect hardly visible to the naked eye, placed it on a blade of grass and hung it by the window of his study. He then took up a position at the end of the room and sat there day after day staring at the insect. At first, he could hardly see it, but after ten days he began to fancy that it was slightly bigger.

For three years he hardly left his study. Then one day he perceived that the insect by the window was as big as a horse. "I've done it!" he exclaimed.

This time the teacher was sufficiently impressed to say, "Well done!"

Chi Ch'ang soon became a master of archery, and no feat of bowmanship now seemed beyond his powers. He seemed close to the achievement of his ambition, but with an unpleasant jolt he realized that one obstacle remained: so long as the master Wei Fei lived, Chi Ch'ang could never call himself the greatest archer in the world.

Walking through the fields one day, Chi Ch'ang caught sight of Wei Fei far in the distance. Without a moment's hesitation he raised his bow, fixed an arrow, and took aim. His old master, however, had sensed what was happening and in a flash had also notched an arrow. Both men fired at the same moment. Their arrows collided halfway and fell together to the ground. The strange duel continued until the master's quiver was empty, but one arrow still remained with the pupil. "Now is my chance!" muttered Chi Ch'ang who immediately aimed the final arrow. Seeing this, Wei Fei broke off a twig from a thorn-bush beside him, and as the arrow sped towards his heart he flicked the point sharply with the tip of one of the thorns and brought it to the ground at his feet.

"My friend," said Wei Fei, "I have now, as you realize, transmitted to you all the knowledge of archery that I possess. If you wish to delve further into these mysteries, you must seek the aged master Kan Ying. Compared to his skill our bowmanship is as the puny fumbling of children.

After months of arduous climbing, Chi Ch'ang reached the cave where dwelt Kan Ying and announced to the old man, "I have come to find out if I am as great an archer as I believe." And without waiting for a reply, he notched an arrow, aimed at a flock of migrating birds, and brought down five birds all at once.

The old man smiled and said, "But this is mere shooting with bow and arrow. Have you not yet learned to shoot without shooting? Come with me."

Chi Ch'ang followed him in silence to the edge of a great cliff. When he glanced down his eyes became blurred, and his head began to spin. Meanwhile the master Kan Ying ran lightly on to a narrow ledge which jutted straight out over the precipice, and turning round said, "Now show me your real skill. Come here where I am standing and let me see your bowmanship."

When Chi Ch'ang stepped on the ledge it began to sway slightly to and fro. He tried to notch an arrow, but soon he felt that he was going to lose his balance. He lay down on the ledge clutching its edges firmly with his fingers. His legs shook and the perspiration flowed from his whole body.

The old man laughed, reached out his hand and helped Chi Ch'ang down. Jumping on to it himself he said, "Allow me, sir, to show you what archery really is."

"What about your bow?" asked Chi Ch'ang.

"My bow?" said the old man laughing. "So long as one requires bow and arrow one is still at the periphery of the art. Real archery dispenses with both bow and arrow."

Directly above their heads a single kite was wheeling in the sky. The hermit looked up at it and Chi Ch'ang followed his gaze. So high was the bird that even to his sharp eyes it looked like a small sesame seed. Kan Ying notched an invisible arrow on an incorporeal bow, drew the string to its full extension, and released it. The next moment the kite stopped flapping its wings and fell like a stone to the ground.

For nine years Chi Ch'ang stayed in the mountains with the old hermit. What disciplines he underwent during this time none ever knew.

When in the tenth year he returned home, all were amazed at the change in him. His former resolute and arrogant countenance had disappeared; in its place had come the look of a simpleton. His old teacher, Wei Fei, came to visit him and said after a single glance, "Now I see that you have indeed become an expert! Such as I are no longer worthy ever to touch your feet."

The inhabitants of his city hailed Chi Ch'ang as the greatest archer in the world and impatiently awaited the wonderful feats which he would not doubt soon display. But Chi Ch'ang did nothing to satisfy their expectations. The great poplar bow which he had taken with him on his journey he evidently had left behind. When someone asked him to explain he answered in a languid tone, "The ultimate stage of activity is inactivity; the ultimate stage of speaking is to refrain from speech; the ultimate in shooting is not to shoot."

Chi Ch'ang grew old. More and more he seemed to have entered the state in which both mind and body look no longer to things outside, but exist by themselves in restful and elegant simplicity. His stolid face divested itself of every vestige of expression; no outside force could disturb his complete impassiveness.

It was rare now for him to speak, and presently one could no longer tell whether or not he still breathed. In the evening of his life he no longer knew the difference between 'this' and 'that'. The kaleidoscope of sensory impressions no longer concerned him; for all he cared, his eye might have been an ear, his ear a nose, his nose a mouth.

Of his last year, the story is told that one day he visited a friend's house and saw lying on a table a vaguely familiar utensil whose name he could, however, not recall. He turned to his friend and said, "Pray tell me: that object on your table -- what is it called, and for what is it used?"

The friend stammered out in an awe-struck tone, "Oh, master. You must indeed be the greatest master of all times. Only so can you have forgotten the bow -- both its name and its use!"

It was said that for some time after this in the city, painters threw away their brushes, musicians broke the strings of their instruments, and carpenters were ashamed to be seen with their rules.

15 █

THE MAGIC OF ZEN

Once there was a very rich magician who had a great many sheep. But at the same time this magician was very mean. He did not want to hire shepherds, nor did he want to erect a fence about the pasture where his sheep were grazing. The sheep consequently often wandered into the forest, fell into ravines, and so on, and above all they ran away, for they knew that the magician wanted their flesh and skins and this they did not like.

At last, the magician found a remedy. He HYPNOTIZED his sheep and suggested to them first of all that they were immortal and that no harm was being done to them when they were skinned, that, on the contrary, it would be very good for them and even pleasant; secondly, he suggested that the magician was a GOOD MASTER who loved his flock so much that he was ready to do anything in the world for them; and in the third place, he suggested to them that if anything at all were going to happen to them it was not going to happen just then, at any rate not that day, and therefore they had no need to think about it. Further, the magician suggested to his sheep that they were not sheep at all; to some of them he suggested that they were lions, to others that they were eagles, to others that they were men, and to others that they were magicians.

And after this all his cares and worries about the sheep came to an end. They never ran away again but quietly awaited the time when the magician would require their flesh and their skins. George Gurdjieff loved this parable very much. His whole philosophy is contained in this small parable. And this parable represents man in the ordinary state of unconsciousness.

~ Osho: The Secret of Secrets, Vol 1 ~

Bill Maher has said that religions are the marketing of a product that basically doesn't exist. Up to some extent, he is right. Down the ages, religions have taught people to believe in absurd things which are unscientific. The weirdest thing religions have conditioned in the mind of human beings is that just by being borne in any religion, you become religious. If someone is born in a Christian family and fills a form where his religion is asked, he will write Christianity. The same is the case with Hinduism, Islam and other religions. This is total crap. You can't be borne into a religion; the religion has to be borne out of you! One becomes a good man not because of his birth and beliefs. One becomes so by actually doing great deeds. One becomes religious by looking into the inner self and realizing the mysteries hidden inside.

Why do you worship great people? Because they did great deeds. Religions give you a substitute for those great deeds. They give you rituals. They say that you don't need to do anything purposeful; all you need is to fulfil the rituals. Just go to this worship place every Sunday, and your work is done. They say just do this ritual or that ritual, and your work is done. Just see the sheer stupidity of such beliefs. Suppose Buddha hadn't work hard on meditation and merely have gone to temples once in a while on some festive occasion, would he have become a Buddha? No!

Ordinary people have some kind of inertia for remaining mediocre. They don't want to come out of their comfort zones. Religions make them live in their comfort zone by giving them stupid beliefs. Hence there are so many followers of each and every religion in the world, and yet religion is missing from the world.

Imagine a garden where only one or two flowers bloomed and rest all the trees remained infertile. The same is the case with humanity. If by merely believing in a particular faith system, the world would have become full of Jesus, or Buddha or Lao Tzu, then yes, we could have said that just having faith is enough. But look at the world around you? Do you see many such great men? No! This simply means that all these so-called religions are phony. Someone has said that the only Christian in the world was crucified. This is right up to some extent.

Only those people who come out of their comfort zone and remain unattracted towards these phony religions realize the true potential within them. The real mystery is hidden inside us. That has to be uncovered through meditation. No one can do it for you. Only you can do it. Once that truth is realized, one comes to realize the magic of life. Then even the mundane life becomes a blessing. You don't need any kind of weed or marijuana to experience that blessing. It comes from within.

In his book Treasury of the forests of ancestors, Satyavayu writes the accounts of a monk Dongshan who later on initiated the Caodong school of Zen. Dongshan was studying Zen with Master Guishan. Dongshan had a question regarding whether a non-sentient being can expound the truth. Master Guishan asked him to visit another Zen Master Yunyan. Under the guidance of Yunyan, finally, Dongshan awakened to his own inner truth, and then he realized that everything around him was bringing bliss to him. So, he wrote his enlightenment couplets:

"How wondrous! How incredible!
The teaching of the non-sentient is beyond conception.

If you listen with your ears, you can't understand.
When you hear with the eyes, then you'll see directly."

Such is the magic of Zen. That experience is a mystery. No one can give it to you. If it could be given, then once Buddha was enlightened, he could have given to everyone else in the world, and the whole world would have become enlightened. You have to experience it in your own meditation.

OTHERS

16

VIMANA

"As we acquire more knowledge, things do not become more comprehensible, but more mysterious."

~ Will Durant ~

In 212 BC Emperor Chi Huang Ti, who built the famous Great Wall of China, ordered to destroy all ancient Chinese texts. There was a great library in Alexandria, Egypt, where thousands of ancient books pertaining to philosophy, history, science and religions were stored. Unfortunately, few fanatic Christians purposely destroyed the library in the third century AD. In 1193 AD came a marauding army of Turks under the leadership of Bakthiyar Khilji. They looted Nalanda (a place in India), and thousands of monks were burnt alive. The great library at Nalanda was put on fire, and its massive collection of books and manuscripts were burnt, which continued to burn for few months. Due to such unfortunate misdeeds of fanatics, we have lost quite a bit of information about the technologies of the past. Yet whatever few pieces of stuff we have from our history are enough to surprise you.

Valmiki Ramayana is a great epic of Hinduism which talks about Pushpak Vimana. Vimana is an aircraft or flying saucer. There are scriptures of vimanas in Hinduism. The stories of vimanas given in ancient Hindu scriptures were considered to be a myth. But there are many ancient carvings that suggest that Gods used to come to vimana to meet human beings. The ancient aliens' theorists suggest that the world was visited by extra-terrestrial in special chariots, and those aliens were considered to be God by human beings.

There are many humongous megalithic monuments in the world. In Peru, there are thousands of years old Nazca lines that span miles. They can't be seen from the earth but can be seen only from the aircraft. The mainstream scientists suggest that aeroplanes were not available then. But ancient aliens theorists believe that extra-terrestrials used to come in their spacecraft, and these mysterious sites were used as landing stations.

We can't be sure how true it is, but it is fascinating!

17

ALIEN ABDUCTION

"People who've had any genuine spiritual experience always know that they don't know. They are utterly humbled before mystery. They are in awe before the abyss of it all, in wonder at eternity and depth, and a Love, which is incomprehensible to the mind."

~ Richard Rohr ~

In Puranas, the ancient Hindu scriptures, there are stories that Gods came to earth and abducted human beings. For example, in Narasimha Purana, Chapter 63, Indra, the king of an alien planet called Devloka, went to Mount Kailasa. There he saw the wife of Kubera and abducted her.

These stories look mythical. But it appears that it has some facticity in such stories too. In 1961, an American couple Barney and Betty Hill, were living in Portsmouth, New Hampshire. On the 19th of September 1961, they were driving back to Portsmouth from a vacation in Niagara Falls and Montreal. They saw a strange flying saucer and few weird people coming out of that saucer. So, they started driving their car. But soon, they became unconscious. When they woke up, they didn't remember what had happened to them.

After three years, they were hypnotized by doctors to find out what had happened to them. Bills recalled that they were abducted by the aliens, and all sort of strange experiments were performed on them. Betty had seen the aliens inserted a probe into her belly button. Barney even claimed that he was forced to provide a sample of his sperm. While Barney died soon, Betty continued to live till 2004. She gave interviews to many TV shows. She was even invited for a lie detector test, which she passed with flying colours!

The incident came to be called "The Hill Abduction". Their story was adapted into the best-selling 1966 book The Interrupted Journey and the 1975 television film The UFO Incident.

This was just the beginning of the onset of several such cases of alien abductions. On the 5th of November 1975, Travis Walton was working in a forest near Snowflake, Arizona. While riding in a truck with six of his co-workers, they encountered a saucer-shaped object hovering over the ground approximately 110 feet away. Those crafts were making a high-pitched buzz. After he left the truck and approached the object, a beam of light suddenly appeared from the craft and knocked him unconscious. The other six men were frightened and supposedly drove away. Later on, he awoke in a hospital-like room, being observed by three short, bald creatures. He claimed that he fought with them until a human wearing a helmet led Walton to another room, where he blacked out as three other humans put a clear plastic mask over his face. Walton has claimed he remembers nothing else until he found himself walking along a highway five days later, with the flying saucer departing above him.

He even passed the lie detector test. Later on, in 1978, Walton wrote a book about his abduction titled 'The Walton Experience'. The book was adapted into the 1993 film 'Fire in the Sky'.

There are many more such cases. In fact, there is a case where the abductee, who was a pregnant lady, said that her foetus was removed by the aliens!

Ancient astronauts' theorists have believed that aliens have always been visiting our planet time and again. The pioneer of this field is Erich Von Daniken. His book 'Chariots of the Gods' has many followers who believe in Aliens, UFOs, and Extra-terrestrials. They believe that the ancient technologies which remained unexplained can only be understood by believing in aliens. There must have been an intelligent race who imparted their knowledge to human beings. Some of them might have been mischievous too and did harm to us as well!

Since he published his book 'Chariots of the Gods' in 1994, many rival or complementary theories about similar subjects have been in publications. Another controversial theory was written by Robert Bauval and Adrian Gilbert in their book 'The Orion Mystery. They observed that the three pyramids at Giza correlate exactly with the placement of the three belt stars of Orion. Further research suggests that there are other monuments in the world located far away from the pyramids of Giza, which correspond to points of the Orion constellation. Their theory is termed 'The Orion Theory'. This theory says that the Ancient Egyptians were descended from alien visitors. It suggests that the alien visitors originated from a planet in the Orion constellation.

Though these theories have been vastly criticized by the mainstream scientists, the forefather of all these types of ideas, Daniken himself, is not bitter about other people's doubt. His book Chariots of the Gods became an instant bestseller in the United States and later across the globe. Since then, he has written dozens of books and sold millions of copies of his work. He enjoys travelling. He has appeared on many television programmes talking about his theories.

Recently a documentary series 'Ancient Aliens' was aired on television, and it was a super hit as well.

Like all theories, Daniken's theory, too, has believers and critics. In the book '100 Strangest Mysteries', Matt Lamy writes:

"Perhaps the mystery in this story is nothing to do with aliens and ancient civilizations, but with how one man created an enormous industry and following based on a **theory with dubious foundations?"**

18

ARTIFICIAL INTELLIGENCE

"Alas! The world is full of enormous lights & mysteries, and the man shuts them from himself with one small hand."

~ Zen Proverb ~

Artificial Intelligence is a term that used to be a field of academic research. Now it has become a common everyday area of knowledge. It signifies any machine or system which has some sort of intelligence. It means any machine which can learn through experience. As and by the machine is used, its performance improves. This happens by collecting a large scale of data. As and by the machine is used, data is gathered and based on the data, the system takes the appropriate next steps.

There are several applications of Artificial Intelligence in our daily lives. A common example is Netflix. Netflix keeps on monitoring the usage by various users. Based on their interests, it shows different thumbnails for the same movie to its different users. A user who mostly watches a horror movie will see a cruel or gruesome thumbnail, whereas another user who mostly watches romantic movies will see a romantic thumbnail for the same movie. Netflix uses artificial intelligence techniques to do so.

Another example can be Youtube. Based on the activities of various users, it shows different kinds of advertisements to different users. Displaying expensive phone advertisements to a student will be of no use. Similarly, showing academic books advertisement to a businessman will be of no use. Traditional programming can't customise its ads automatically according to the user. It can show the same sets of advertisements to all the users.

Similarly, many of you might have seen or even used a vacuum mop robot. It walks around in the room and automatically scans the map of the house. As it gets struct to a wall or any other obstacle, it gathers the information to build an accurate map. Next time it will not get stuck to the same wall again. All this happens through data gathering and artificial intelligence.

Now let us go back to ancient scriptures. In the Ramacharitmanasa of Tulsidas, there is an extraordinary incidence. Rama was ready to fight with the demon king Ravana. One night, Ravana, the ten-headed demon, was enjoying a music program along with his wife, Mandodari.

When Rama came to know, he strung his bow and fitted an arrow to the string and left it. What happens after this is wonderful. I am quoting the verses from the scripture's book 7, couplet (Doha) 13:

Chatra mukuṭa tāṭaṅka taba hatē ēkahīṁ bāna.

Saba kēṁ dēkhata mahi parē maramu na kō'ū jāna.

Means:

Using a single shaft, the Lord then struck Ravan's umbrella and crowns as well as (Ravana's wife) Mandodari's eardrops, which fell to the ground before the very eyes of all; but none could know the mystery.

The next verse is even more interesting:

Asa kautuka kari rāma sara prabisē'u ā'i niṣaṅga.

Rāvana sabhā sasaṅka saba dēkhi mahā rasabhaṅga.

Means:

"Having performed this startling feat Sri Rama's shaft came back and dropped into his quiver again. And everybody in Ravana's assembly was alarmed to see this great interruption in his revelry."

Generally, those who try to analyse such stories from the standpoint of science say that this is merely symbolic mythology. What does it signify? In India, after the death of any person, a 13 days' ritual is performed. In the story also, the arrow destroys 13 things: 10 crowns on the heads of Ravana, two eardrops in the ear of Mandodari and one umbrella. These sums out to be 13. By doing so, Rama warned Ravana of the coming 13 days mourning period to the Lanka!

If you say the same verse to a scientist of the 18th or 19th century, probably he won't believe it. But now, when we know about artificial intelligence and vacuum mop robots, it doesn't seem to be entirely impossible. The arrows were simply artificially intelligent!

19

GENDER CHANGE

"There is a reality even prior to heaven and earth;
Indeed, it has no form, much less a name;
Eyes fail to see it;
It has no voice for ears to detect;
To call it Mind or Buddha violates its nature,
For it then becomes like a visionary flower in the air;
It is not Mind, nor Buddha;
Absolutely quiet, and yet illuminating in a mysterious way,
It allows itself to be perceived only by the clear-eyed."

~ Daio ~

Again, I will take you to some of the Hindu scriptures. In Mahabharata and various Puranas, there is the story of Il. In some books, he is also called by the name Sudyumna. He was the son of Vaivasvata Manu. One day, he goes to a divine grove and suddenly gets transformed into a woman. He becomes Ila and gets married to Budha.

Such stories were called mythology, but now science has developed a lot. A person's gender can be transitioned. A male can be converted into a female and vice versa. Hence, such stories are not totally impossible!

20

DANGEROUS WEAPONS

"If you think there are any verbal formulations that are special mysterious secrets to be transmitted, this is not real Zen. Real Zen has no transmission. It is just a matter of people experiencing it, resulting in their ability to see each other's vision and communicate tacitly."

~ Dahui ~

Greek legends tell the story of Prometheus, who stole the fires from God. Fire could create catastrophe and be used as a weapon in ancient times. Iron has been used as a weapon for long and to mould the iron, one needs fire! Ancient Hindu scriptures talk a lot about dangerous weapons. In the Mahabharata, 46 different types of deadly weapons have been mentioned. It also talks about Brahmastra, The Brahma Weapon. It is a kind of nuclear weapon and can destroy the whole world. One story tells that Arjuna got a deadly weapon called Pashupata from Lord Shiva.

Another story in Mahabharata talks about a weapon hold by Lord Vishnu called Chakra. It is like a guided missile. It can track the destination and hit it. It won't hit any other target!

In Japanese legends, there is a folktale of Amakuni who created the first single-edged longsword with the help of Shinto Gods. Here is the story from Wikipedia:

'One day, Amakuni and his son, Amakura, were standing in the doorway of their shop, watching the Emperor's warriors return from battle. Although having done so on previous occasions, the Emperor did not give Amakuni any sign of recognition. Having always looked upon these gestures as a sign of appreciation for his efforts and hard work, Amakuni suddenly noticed that nearly half of the returning warriors were carrying broken swords.

Determined to make things right, Amakuni and Amakura went about gathering remnants of the swords and examined them. It appeared that the chief reasons for breakage were that the swords had been improperly forged and that the soldiers had struck hard objects, probably armor or other weapons, with them. Once again, the Emperor's subtle yet audible rebuff ran through his mind. Tears filled Amakuni's eyes, and he said to himself, "If they are going to use our swords for such slashing, I shall make one that will not break."

With this vow, Amakuni and his son sealed themselves away in the forge and prayed for seven days and seven nights to the Shinto gods. Amakuni then selected the best iron sand ore he could obtain and refined it into steel. Working without rest, the two worked at their apparently impossible task. Thirty-one days later, Amakuni and his son emerged gaunt and weary from the forge with a single-edged sword with curvature. Undaunted by the other swordsmiths, who believed them to be insane, Amakuni and Amakura ground and polished the new sword.

During the following months, Amakuni and his son continued with their work, forging many types of improved swords. In the following spring, there was another war. Again, the samurai returned, and as they passed by, he counted over thirty-one swords with perfect, intact blades. As the Emperor passed, he smiled and said, "You are an expert swordmaker. None of the swords you have made failed in this battle." Amakuni rejoiced and once more felt that life was full and joyous.

It is not known when Amakuni died, though legend has it that he gained immortality from the large amount of blood shed from the blades he created.'

We have learnt about nuclear reactions only in the past few centuries. How could ancient people know about such a devastating weapon? Ancient astronaut theorists suggest that they got this knowledge from extra-terrestrials. They suggest that getting the weapons from Gods can have only one meaning, and that is they got it from aliens!

21

SUDDEN COMBUSTION

"People have a hard time letting go of their suffering. They prefer suffering that is familiar to the unknown."

~ Thich Nhat Hanh ~

Hindu scriptures talk about a vital life force called Prana. Though it is used synonymously for the breath, yet scriptures say that breath has a life force, and it is that life force which Prana.

A long time ago, people used to view objects as matters. But later on, science found that matter has a lot of energy. If nuclear reactions take place, they might produce a vast burst of energy. The same is the case with human beings too. We, too, have a lot of energy that we don't recall.

In Hinduism, there is the story of Sati, the wife of Lord Shiva. One day, when Sati's father insulted Lord Shiva, Sati became very angry. Out of anger, she ignited meditative energy from her body and then let her body burn into ashes. This story has come in many Puranas (ancient scriptures of Hinduism). In the Ramacharitmanasa of Tulsidasa, he says:

"As kahi jog agini tanu jara"

Which means, "after saying rude words to her father she burnt her body in Yoga fire."

Ordinarily, people will consider it to be a mythological story. How can one burn spontaneously without any external fuel source? So, traditional scholars say that this is merely a symbolic story where fire signifies anger. They say that Sati might have been burnt by an external fire source, and since she was rageful at her father, it is said that she burnt in her own fire. Whenever scholars see anything which they can't explain, they say that it is mythology or merely symbolism. By calling the incident symbolism, they mean to say that the actual incident didn't happen in the same way as it is mentioned; rather, the incidents are merely symbols of some deep philosophical meaning. By saying so, they save themselves from finding the science behind such stories.

Understand this! We know about Pythagoras theorem. It says that in a right-angled triangle, a squared + b squared = c squared. If someone starts to say that Pythagoras Theorem is not true, rather it is merely a symbolism. Here Pythagoras wanted to say that when a boy and a girl fall in love together and decide to get married and marry, then with each other co-operation both of them can give birth to a child c. It is merely a symbolism, and Pythagoras theorem doesn't exist. What will you call such a commentator? The symbolic explanation is alright, but Pythagoras theorem is scientific truth in itself.

The same is the case here too. Since people are not able to explain the self-burning of Sati's body, they say it is a mythological story. But in the past century, few very weird phenomena have been observed which have intrigued scientists.

Mary Hardy Reeser (1884 – 1951) used to live in St. Petersburg, Florida. On July 2, 1951, Reeser's landlady, Pansy Carpenter, arrived with a telegram to see her. Since Reeser didn't open the door, she tried to open herself. Trying the door, she found the metal doorknob to be uncomfortably warm to be touched. She then called the police.

Reeser's remains, which were largely ashes, were found among the remains of a chair in which she had been sitting. Only part of her left foot (which was wearing a slipper) and her backbone remained, along with her skull. Plastic household objects at a distance from the seat of the fire were slightly deformed due to the heat.

Reeser's skull had survived and was found among the ashes but shrunken to the size of an orange. No evidence of anything which could have ignited her body was seen nearby.

Similarly, 92 years old physician Dr J. Irving Bentley used to live in Coudersport, Pennsylvania (USA). On December 5 1966, a meter reader Don Gosnell went to do the meter check at Dr Bentley's house. Since no one opened the door, he let himself in because he smelt a sweet smell and a cloud of light blue smoke coming out of the house. When he went inside, he was left shocked to see the scene. Whole body of Dr Bentley was burnt into ash. Only the left leg and the shoe remained unburnt. All other parts of the body were burnt into ash. Experts explored the house but couldn't find any source of fire there. Thus, they concluded that it was a case of Sudden Human Combustion where the body was burnt without any apparent external source of ignition. The weirdest part was that the smell coming out of the body was not foul; rather, it was a sweet smell!

For a long time, Sudden Human Combustion (SHC) has been considered to be pseudoscientific by mainstream researchers. But such incidents have occurred many times in the past.

Michael Faherty (1934-2010) used to live in Galway, a county in Ireland. On December 22, 2010, Faherty's neighbour, Mr Mannion, was awakened by the smoke alarm coming out of Faherty's house. He went outside to find smoke coming out of Faherty's house. First, he tried to knock on the door of Faherty, but since he didn't respond, he had to rouse the local residents and call the fire brigade.

His body was found lying on the back and burnt to death. There was no apparent cause of ignition nearby.

In 2011, the west Galway coroner, Dr Ciaran McLoughlin, inquired into the death of Faherty and concluded that it was the case of Sudden Human Combustion!

While mainstream scientists deny the possibility of SHC, there are some sceptics who have come up with many alternative theories. Scientist and research Brian J. Ford have suggested that ketosis, which might be possibly caused by alcoholism or low-carb dieting, produces acetone. Acetone is highly flammable and could therefore lead to apparently spontaneous combustion.

Larry E. Arnold has written a book 'ABLAZE! The Mysterious Fires of Spontaneous Human Combustion' which was published in 1995. In that book, he proposed a pseudoscientific new subatomic particle, which he called "pyrotron". According to him, that particle is susceptible to Sudden Human Combustion. But he has not provided any evidence for the existence of such particles.

So, in short, the reason for the Sudden Human Combustion is still a mystery waiting to be solved.

Upanishads are supposed to be one of the highest forms of wisdom by Hindus. In one of the Upanishads called Prashnopanishada, it is said that there are five kinds of prana fire dwelling in human bodies. Science suggests that the human body, too, works on electricity. Our brain uses electricity to send signals to various parts of the body.

In 1895 there was a girl, Jenny Morgan. After she got 13 years old, her body suddenly started to generate electric shock. A scientist touched Jenny to examine her and got a high voltage shock, and remained unconscious for hours. Once, she lifted a cat in her arms. But the affection of Jenny for the cat turned out to be fatal for the cat!

There are very few such cases of people who were live electric powerhouse. It appears that if somehow that electric flow is disrupted, the body can either harm others through electric shock or can burn itself to ashes.

There is another mysterious case of Therese Neumann (1898-1962), who was a German mystic. It has been reported that from 1923 until her death in 1962, she didn't have any food or water. She still survived without any health problems. It appears that there is a source of energy within us, which somehow remains unavailable to ordinary people. If that energy source is activated in the wrong way, it might cause body combustion!

Now, if we come back to the story of Sati, can we definitely say that the story is a myth, and a body can't ignite by itself? Can we say with 100% surety that the story is a myth and such an incident never happened? Probably not!

22

MYSTERIOUS PEOPLE

"The familiar, precisely because it is familiar, remains unknown."

~ Hegel ~

Have you heard about 'Bible John'? He is an unidentified serial killer. He used to be in Glasgow, Scotland, United Kingdom. Between 1968 and 1969, he murdered three young brunette women between the ages of 25 and 32. Surprisingly all his victims were menstruating at the time of murder! The suspect was said to be frequently quoting from the Bible, and thus he was named as 'Bible John'. Over five thousand suspects were interrogated, but ultimately the criminal was not to be caught, and the case remains unsolved to date.

Many murderers were never identified. They lived among us like other ordinary human beings. We don't even know their name.

I will take you again to Ramacharitmanasa of Tulsidas. When Rama, along with his wife Sita and brother Lakshmana, was in exile, a mysterious person came to meet them. He seemed to be a devotee of Rama. After meeting Rama, he returned. Below are the words of Ramacharitmanasa, Book 2, near Verse 110:

'In the meantime, there arrived an ascetic who was an embodiment of spiritual glow, Young in years and charming in appearance. His

ways were unknown to the poet; he was attired in the garb of a recluse and was devoted to Rama in thought word and deed.

His eyes were wet with tears and a thrill ran through his body when he came to recognize his beloved Deity (Sri Rama). He fell prostrate on the ground and the state of his body and mind could not be described in words.

Thrilling all over with emotion, Sri Rama pressed him to His bosom, as though a pauper had found a philosopher's stone. Everyone who saw them suggested as though love, on the one hand and the supreme Reality, on the other, embraced each other in living form.'

It appears that Rama was affectionate towards the ascetic. But surprisingly, his name is not mentioned in the scripture. The scholars of Ramayana have given various theories about him. Some say these verses were not present in the original book and were a later addition, while others believe they were present in the original text because they are present in the ancient manuscripts. Despite abundant theories, when the author himself doesn't mention his name, all the efforts to identify that person is futile in my view. Perhaps the author wanted to tell us that many people in the world are remarkable yet unknown. We can never know their name and identify them!

23

CONCLUDING REMARKS...

"To know that you do not know is the best.
To pretend to know when you do not know is a disease.
Recognizing this disease as a disease is to be free of it."

~ Tao Te Ching, Lao Tzu ~

In August 1977, an Ohio State University radio telescope detected an unusual pulse of radiation for 37 seconds from somewhere near the constellation Sagittarius. It was so mysteriously startling that an astronomer monitoring the data scrawled "Wow!" on the telescope's printout. The scientists kept on waiting, but such a signal was not received again. The signal was within the band of radio frequencies where transmissions are internationally banned on Earth. Furthermore, natural sources of radiation from space usually cover a wider range of frequencies. As the nearest star in that direction is 220 million light-years away, it is implausible that the signal was originating from there. The most plausible explanation was that there must be intelligent aliens with a very powerful transmitter that would have created it. However, the source of the signal remains a mystery to date.

There are a lot of mysteries that have still not been solved. Those mysteries open our eyes to existence. They make us realize that there are a lot of things to be explored. Knowing about those mysteries helps a student of Zen. Meditation is a path of the unknown. Only those people can meditate who are ready to take a journey into the unknown. Before meditating, no one knows what he will experience during meditation. One person can see darkness during meditation, whereas another person can see white or blue light. There is no guarantee of what you will see. A person who wants all the answers in the beginning before starting the journey can never progress in the path.

A so-called religious person keeps on deceiving himself by pretending that he knows everything. He knows who created the world. He knows about heaven and hell. They can't say that they don't know. And they don't say that whatever is their belief is merely a belief. They pretend that they know it. This pretention has created phony religious people in the world who are devoid of the true religious experience. Only that person can go far on the journey of Zen; who knows that he doesn't know. He doesn't pretend to be a knower. He is happy to remain ignorant until he gets a first-hand experience.

Start working on the path by understanding that you don't know, and you will experience what all the Buddhas have experienced. In this book, we have talked about the mysteries of the external world. But the real secret lies within you. Eckhart Tolle has said that you don't have a life; you are life. Even if you know the secrets of the whole universe and your inner truth remains unexplored, it would be of no use. When we realise our inner self, or maybe 'no-self,' we reach home!

I wish you a zensational mysterious journey on the path of Tao!

BIBLIOGRAPHY

1. The Zen Teaching of Bodhidharma, Translated by Red Pine
2. Records of Yunmen, Tr by Urs App
3. Zen's Chinese Heritage by Andy Ferguson
4. Records of the Transmission of the Lamp (Jingde Chuandeng Lu, Vol 1-6) by Daoyuan, translated by Randolph S. Whitfield
5. The Original Teachings of Ch'an Buddhism by Chang Ching Yuan
6. Buddha Root Farm by Hsuan Hua
7. Buddhism of Wisdom and Faith for Pure Land Principles and Practice by Dharma Master Thich-Thien-Tam
8. Reincarnation: Exceptional Cases of Past Life Memories by Eirik Leivsson
9. Zen, The Quantum Leap from Mind To No-Mind by Osho
10. The Dark Side of Japan by Antony Cummins
11. Zen Flesh Zen Bones by Paul Reps & Nyogen Sengaki
12. The Parinirvana Sutra
13. Meditating with Koans by Thomas Cleary
14. The Spirit of Zen by Sam van Schaik
15. The Secret of Secrets. Vol. 1 by Osho
16. Ramacharitmanasa of Goswami Tulsidasa
17. Narasimha Purana
18. Mahabharata
19. 100 Strangest Mystery by Matt Lamy

20. 'The Stories about the Foremost Elder Nuns' translated by Anandajoti Bhikkhu

21. 'The Archer' by Nakashima Ton

22. The Great Chronicle of Buddhas by Ven. Mingun Sayadaw

23. A Foundations: An Illustrated Guide to Mathematics: From Creating the Pyramids to Exploring Infinity by Anne Rooney

24. Treasury of the Forest of Ancestors by Satyavayu

25. Time Slips: Real Stories of Time Travel by Katherine Fletcher

26. Ablaze! The Mysterious Fires of Spontaneous Human Combustion by Larry E. Arnold

27. Web Resources:

- http://www.buddhism.org/seoam-honggeun-1917-2003/
- Images taken from Wikipedia
- https://www.keithhearne.com/wp-content/uploads/2010/06/THREE-PREMONITIONS.pdf
- https://www.cureus.com/articles/19443-the-eye-of-horus-the-connection-between-art-medicine-and-mythology-in-ancient-egypt
- 'Archaeoacoustic Analysis of the Hal Saflieni Hypogeum in Malta' by Prof.agg. Paolo Debertolis and Dr. Fernando Augusto Coimbra, Centro Português de Geo-históiria e Pré-História, Lisboa, Portugal (https://www.researchgate.net/publication/282480957_Archaeoacoustic_Analysis_of_the_Hal_Saflieni_Hypogeum_in_Malta)